WHEN YOU LOVE SOMEONE

Winter Lake

RHIAN CAHILL

Rhian Cahill

When You Love Someone
Winter Lake
By Rhian Cahill

For more information visit:
www.rhiancahill.com

Love Me Like You Do
Love The Way You Are
When You Love Someone
Let Me Love You
Wild Rush Of Love

WHEN YOU LOVE SOMEONE
WINTER LAKE BOOK 3

When it comes to love the tough guys always go down the hardest.

Sophie Collins is used to the adoring attention from her fans but the overzealous one who cooked her a meal and left it—with heating instructions—in her fridge has gone too far. No longer safe in her own house, she hops a plane and travels halfway around the world.

He was sent to bring her home safe. But from the minute Sophie falls into Stone's arms he knows she's not the only thing in danger. He's a hardened warrior trained to kill with his bare hands and one too sweet too young pop singer is bringing him to his knees.

If he can't keep her safe and neutralize the threat he stands to lose more than his client. He'll lose his heart.

For all the boys who have stolen a kiss on the Ferris wheel. And for those who like a good yarn.

CHAPTER 1

6AM SATURDAY - SYDNEY, Australia

"Fuck. This guy has a serious hard-on for our girl."

Stone grunted in acknowledgement and glowered at the four walls boxing them in.

Every square inch—including the ceiling—was covered with photos of Sophie Collins.

She was a good-looking woman—hell, she was hot—and you couldn't hold it against a man for admiring the sexy songstress, but these pictures made Stone's gut churn and his blood boil.

This went beyond normal admiration. It wasn't the work of a besotted teenage boy or overzealous fan. What was spread out in front of them took this case from fanatical follower to obsessed stalker in the blink of an eye.

Something familiar snagged his gaze and he leaned in close for a better look. Recognition slammed into him. Sophie's bed. "Holy shit. He's got a feed into her house."

"What?" Ford Moreland charged over, shouldered him out of the way and bent to study the picture Stone pointed at. "Get someone in her fucking house right now, Aiden," his boss yelled. "I want whatever link this cock has shut down."

Stone liked working for Aiden and Ford Moreland. The brothers might be a little rough around the edges most of the time, but he appreciated that there was no beating around the bush, no bullshit, no sugar-coating. If a job needed doing, it got done ASAP.

Their company, Landlocked, dealt with all forms of security—high-tech systems for buildings, computer networks, etcetera—and Stone's favorite, and area of expertise: personal protection.

Except they hadn't done a great job of protecting Sophie Collins.

She was missing.

Twenty hours and counting since anyone had lain eyes on her.

Chip burst through the shed doorway behind them, laptop in hand. "You're not gonna like this, boss."

Ford laughed, the sound harsh and humorless as he turned to face the other man. "Yeah, 'cause I'm liking what I've seen so far." Blowing out a breath, he nodded. "Give it to me."

"He piggy-backed our system to get a visual inside her house. He also hijacked our trackers. That's why all the feeds went dead yesterday. I reactivated everything but nothing's pinging. Yet."

"Jesus fucking Christ. Who *is* this guy?" Ford growled. "I want a name and I want it *now*."

Stone knew how Ford felt. He'd wanted the guy's name a week ago when they thought they were dealing with nothing more than an overzealous fan.

If the fact the owner of this property, Henry Whittaker, appeared to be a ghost hadn't clued them in then the shed they stood in blew that notion to smithereens.

They'd either underestimated this guy or he'd escalated one thousand percent in the last week.

He hated to admit it, but they'd miscalculated. They weren't dealing with a simple fan gone rogue—they never had been.

They had to get a handle on the situation. Fast.

The bastard had dodged them at every turn though. Hell, the fucker had not only gotten inside Sophie's house on their watch, he'd stuck around long enough to make himself a meal, for Christ's sake.

Even left a plate with reheating instructions—among other *gifts*—for Sophie, all while avoiding being caught on camera.

In the last twenty hours, everything had gone pear-shaped. Their client was missing and their target seemed to be the invisible man. He couldn't remember a more FUBAR job.

If they didn't find Sophie soon, he feared this guy would—if he hadn't already—and Stone didn't think the prick had anything pleasant planned for the pretty pop star.

The only thing they had going in their favor was Sophie had left her house alone. She appeared rushed and a little freaked out but she'd definitely been by herself when Landlocked's security cameras taped her lugging a suitcase through her front door.

But with her location still unknown they couldn't protect her, and with the evidence in front of them Stone had to acknowledge she needed their protection far more than any of them had thought.

"Any intel on where she is now?" Stone asked. If anyone could track the un-trackable, it was Chip.

"I might have the answer to that." Aiden strode into the shed, eyes focused on the tablet in his hand. "But Ford isn't gonna like it."

Ford snorted. "Oh, yeah, because Ford's in love with every damn fucking thing so far."

Stone's lips twitched. His boss always managed to put a smile on his face in spite of whatever shit-hole they found themselves in. Ford's warped sense of humor had saved their sanity on more than one job over the years.

"First, this guy isn't as smart as we think. Jack's grabbing the genius behind the hacking now," Aiden offered.

"For fuck's sake," Stone cursed. This shit just kept getting better and better. "There are *two* people involved?"

"Explain," Ford growled over Stone's words.

"Give me a sec…" Aiden tapped away.

Stone was on the verge of grabbing his boss by the throat when Aiden spoke again.

"Ah, there. Sophie Collins hopped a plane for LA about

four hours after we lost her. Here's the part you're *really* not going to like."

Stone had had enough. "Cut the BS and spit it out!"

His temples throbbed and his jaw ached from grinding his back teeth. He hated feeling useless and right now he felt downright impotent.

They needed to find Sophie Collins *now*.

"According to our perp's email he boarded the same aircraft under the name Henry Whittaker."

"He was on her fucking plane?" Stone exploded. The pounding in his head a moment ago was nothing compared to the thunder roaring through him now. How could they have screwed the situation up so badly?

"Easy there." Ford gripped Stone's shoulder, digging his fingers in hard, no doubt to keep him in place. Satisfied Stone wasn't going anywhere, Ford nodded at his brother. "What else, Aiden?"

Aiden eyed Stone for a moment, one eyebrow cocked, before returning his gaze to the information in front of him. "I'm still following the trail but Sophie hired a limo to take her to The Beverly Hilton. She's booked in for a two-week stay. Can't find Henry Whittaker on the guest register."

"How did this non-existent Henry Whittaker get a passport?" Ford aimed the question at Chip. "I want everything you find on this guy and I don't care how you get the information."

Chip nodded and began furiously tapping at the keys of his ever-present laptop.

A gangly teenager—all of sixteen, judging by the fuzz on his chin—stumbled into the shed.

Jack calmly strolled in behind him. "Got the little shit. Had to drag his ass out of bed."

The "little shit" glanced around, eyes widening with each man his gaze landed on. His prominent Adam's apple bobbed up and down his skinny neck as he swallowed.

When he spotted the photos covering the walls, his mouth dropped open and his eyes almost bugged right out of his head. "What the...?" He spun toward the door.

"Whoa." Jack grabbed the waistband of the kid's pants and swung him back around. "Stay right where you are. We are not done."

"But..." The kid's terrified gaze pinged around the room, avoiding eye contact with the men surrounding him.

"What's your name?" Ford asked in a mild tone, but Stone could hear the rage—the urgency—vibrating in each word.

"M-Mike." The kid licked his lips. "I d-don't know anything about t-this. I j-just did what he p-paid me for."

Not bothering to modulate his anger the way his brother had, Aiden stepped forward, got right in the kid's face and demanded, "Who and what?"

"G-G-G-George." The kid hooked a thumb over his shoulder toward the house visible through the busted-off-its-hinges shed door behind him. "H-he lives here."

Aiden arched an eyebrow. "George?"

"Y-yeah." The kid nodded, his Adam's apple bobbing several times, sweat beading on his forehead and upper lip.

"Got a last name?" Ford asked.

"D-D-D-Davis," the kid sputtered.

Stone couldn't decide if the stammering was nerves or a genuine affliction.

Not that it mattered. He didn't care about the kid beyond what he could tell them about Sophie's mysterious stalker.

It chapped Stone's ass to think this kid probably knew more about the guy than they did. Including what he looked like. So far they had three descriptions of Whittaker. If that was even his name.

"How many fucking names does this prick have?" Stone barked, the question aimed at no one in particular.

He could hear his frustration leaching into his voice and tried to rein in his temper but feared he was fighting a losing battle; with every second his annoyance at the situation escalated.

"I've got a bead on five..." Chip murmured as he tapped away on his laptop.

"Five?" Stone asked in disbelief.

"It's irrelevant." Ford turned and faced Stone head-on. "Get on the first flight to LA. Find Sophie. Bring her home. Find Henry/George/whoever-the-fuck-he-is today. If he's touched her, he doesn't take another breath."

Stone's spine snapped straight, his whole body going rigid. He didn't think Ford meant for him to actually terminate the guy. Not really. But he completely understood the seriousness of his boss's words.

This guy would pay for anything and everything he'd done to Sophie Collins.

And it wasn't as though Stone couldn't put the guy

down if necessary. He'd been given kill orders before. And while he'd done his job back then, followed every order to the letter, he'd never once felt the pleasure currently flowing through his veins at the thought of taking someone out.

He'd do his job. Find this guy and take him down.

For Sophie.

"Don't worry, boss. The motherfucker is going down. Hard."

CHAPTER 2

5PM Sunday - Winter Lake, New York, USA

Sophie stared. Blinked. Stared some more. She gave her head a little shake...tipped it to the side and squinted...

Nope, nothing changed. It was still there.

"Oh my god." The words were whispered through parched lips.

She'd somehow found herself in a real-life, living, breathing postcard.

Winter Lake lived up to everything she'd ever expected to find in a sleepy little mountain town in the middle of Nowheresville, America.

She had no idea what the population was but it appeared as though every last one of the people who called Winter Lake home currently wandered down the barricaded main street.

She stood on the fringes of some kind of festival. The biggest giveaway was the Ferris wheel set up in the parkland edging the huge lake on one side of the street.

Sophie frowned.

Unless it was a year-round thing. Surely that big wheel and all those booths weren't permanent fixtures.

Her frown deepened as she pondered the absurdity of that thought.

It was also possible she was hallucinating the whole thing. Tired and stressed, Sophie wouldn't be at all surprised to discover she'd lost her mind.

After hours sitting on the wrong side of the car, driving on the wrong side of the road, her brain had been switched upside down, inside out and back to front.

Thirsty and hungry and cramped, she'd needed to stretch her legs, find some food, and at this late hour, she should probably ask directions to the nearest hotel.

The sun dipped low in the sky, kissing the top of the mountain on the other side of the lake, and unless she found accommodations soon, she'd be sleeping in her rental. Or driving through the night.

Neither option sounded safe or remotely appealing.

First thing on her agenda should definitely be locating a hotel. She glanced up and down the road. Although judging by the size of the main street—suitably named *Lake Front* —she wouldn't find a hotel in Winter Lake.

She'd exited the highway when she'd seen the sign for the town and, as soon as she'd found a spot, parked the convertible she'd rented back in Albany between two utes

—no, wait, this was America, they called them trucks here, didn't they?

Whatever. She was pretty sure her little car would fit in the back of either ute with room to spare, regardless of what they were called.

Sophie admired her sweet ride—unquestionably it had been the wrong vehicle to lease when she wanted to blend in. One more thing she'd messed up.

It seemed she'd been making wrong decisions from the second she'd come home Friday morning to find someone had been in her house.

She sighed and muttered under her breath, "Dammit."

"You lost, love?"

Sophie spun around. And her jaw dropped.

The man who had spoken was as old as time and just as dirty.

He wore a flannel shirt over denim overalls, both liberally splattered with multiple streaks of grease, mud and... eeww...*was that poo?*

In spite of the million or so wrinkles marring his tanned skin, his face was friendly and the smile he flashed her was bright and genuine and set his watery-blue eyes sparkling.

She found herself smiling in return. The most sincere one she'd managed in over a week. "Um, no, I'm not lost. I'm in Winter Lake, right?"

"That you are, missy." He tucked his dirty, gnarled hands into the front bib of his overalls. "You here for the festival?"

"Festival?"

Chuckling, he said, "You didn't think Lake Front Park always looked like that, did you?"

She glanced around. "Ah...well no, I guess not."

"You got family here? Can't place the accent but it sure isn't from around here. Don't reckon I've heard or seen anything as pretty as you in a while either." He scratched his whiskered chin with dirt-crusted fingers. "Can't place who you might belong to though."

Belong to? "Ah, no, I...um..." She needed to blend in. Didn't want anyone to know who she was or why she was here, and the more questions this stranger asked, the tighter her insides coiled. She kept her voice soft, her tone even. "I'm just passing through."

"Well now, that's a shame. The annual Ice Breaker Festival is a sight to see and lots of out-of-towners come in for a looky-loo."

Sophie gazed over at the Ferris wheel and numerous stalls again. It did look inviting and she did need somewhere to stay. Somewhere she could hide until she figured out how the guy following her managed to turn up every place she went.

She'd flown halfway around the world for heaven's sake, and he'd still found her. This tiny town tucked away in the mountains seemed as good as any other to stop, even if only for one night.

She was so damn tired that the thought of stopping filled her with so much relief it made her dizzy.

"Are you sure you don't need help?" the old man asked.

"No, I..." She pulled her gaze from the festival and

returned it to his shrewd blue eyes. "Actually, is there a hotel I could check into?"

"A hotel?" He laughed, the sound deep and rattly in his chest, his large frame shaking as he gave her attire a once-over. "We don't got no fancy hotel unless you're talking about Winter Lake Lodge which used to be an uppity 5-star place in its heyday over on the west side of the lake. We've got a few bed-and-breakfast places too. They usually have a room but with the festival, you'll be plumb outta luck on those."

At this point she'd take anything. A chair in a closet sounded good. "I'm not fussy. Any of those places will do. Could you give me directions from here?"

"You got a car?"

Sophie indicated her red sports car, drawing another crackly laugh from the old guy.

"That there's no car. Not unless you're talking toy cars like the ones my great grandsons push around in the dirt." He shook his head and grinned at her. "You'll be wanting the Lodge. You need to drive that itty-bitty thing down Lake Front thataway then follow the road around the edge of the lake until it meets up with Fire Trail Drive then keep going west. You'll see the Lodge on the right up a little ways. It's a big old building right on the lake, but with the festival, the road is blocked and you have to go around." He tipped his head toward the road behind her, "Jus' head down the road thisaway, take the first right, then again and again, and go left back onto Lake Front."

"Ah, okay. Thanks."

Sophie wasn't quite sure she understood his directions.

She wasn't the best when it came to navigating. Or deter-mining left from right when she was driving on the *correct* side of the road.

Put her on the other side and, well...that was how she'd ended up in Winter Lake, New York, instead of Hidden Peak, New York.

Not that she had any particular reason to go to Hidden Peak. She only needed somewhere she could stay off the grid so she could shake the man who'd followed her all the way to LA from Australia, and Hidden Peak had sounded... well, hidden, like a place no one would hide because it seemed too obvious and that had given her a slight feeling of comfort—safety.

Something she hadn't really felt for days.

She shuddered when she recalled arriving home to find a plated meal with heating instructions in her fridge, her bed scattered with rose petals and a black negligée draped across her pillow, a handwritten note beside it.

"You sure you're okay? I can take you over there if you want."

Sophie snapped out of the distressing memories and forced a smile. "Oh, no. That won't be necessary. I've got it."

She tried to instill as much confidence into her voice and smile as she could. But after spotting the strange man who seemed to pop up everywhere she was for weeks now in the hotel lobby in LA yesterday morning, she was just about out of confidence.

How had he found her?

When she'd left her house and taken an Uber to Sydney

airport, she'd checked several times to be certain no one followed her. She hadn't seen him once—except in her nightmares—since she'd left home. Until yesterday morning.

Thrown into a mad panic when faced with those ice-cold eyes again, she'd raced back to her room, grabbed her bag, and once more headed for the airport.

The woman behind the airline counter had given her a strange look when Sophie had demanded a ticket on the next plane out of LA no matter where it was going.

Albany, New York, had been the destination. And Sophie had been careful to give every person who boarded the plane before her a good long look. She hadn't recognized any of them as the man who appeared to be following her everywhere.

She had no idea who he was, only that whenever she spotted him—and she'd spotted him a lot—a chill dropped over her, her skin crawled, and she had to fight the urge to run and hide.

"Well now, if you get stuck, just holler at the nearest person. They'll help you out. Folks around here are a friendly bunch. No one's a stranger for long in these parts."

That's what Sophie was afraid of. She needed to keep a low profile. She already stood out like a sore thumb with her sporty little car and her outfit.

Everyone here wore jeans or shorts, t-shirts or long sleeved shirts; there were even a few flannel shirts, and boots. Boots of all kinds. Some were scuffed, some looked brand new. Everyone wore boots.

Her four-inch strappy wedge heels weren't small town

at all. And the pretty little floral dress and cute knit cardigan she'd picked up at LAX didn't help. It definitely screamed big city, not small mountain town.

At least she hadn't hit the charts here with much success yet. If she were back home she wouldn't be able to stand on a public street without being recognized.

Here she stood a good chance of going unnoticed completely except for the fact she wasn't a local and clearly didn't fit in. The festival might give her some cover but that would only last as long as the festivities did.

She'd have to be more selective in her wardrobe choices from now on. Not that she had much to choose from. She hadn't repacked after her four day trip to Brisbane. When she'd seen someone had been in her house, she'd grabbed her unpacked bag and called an Uber. Her panicked departure meant nothing appropriate for the mountain climate of North America.

"Miss?"

Snapped from her thoughts she forced another smile and said, "Thank you for your help."

Giving a little wave, she briskly walked to her car, unlocked the door, and climbed inside.

All she wanted to do was lay her head on the steering wheel and cry, but no doubt her Good Samaritan would come over and offer to help again.

Digging deep for the bravado she used every time she stepped out on stage in front of thousands of people, she turned the car on and pulled out into traffic. Not that one car could be considered traffic.

Driving until she reached the first right, she turned and

drove until she found the next one. Turning again, she drove a bit before pulling over and putting the car in park. She gave in to one of her urges, leaned forward, and put her forehead against the wheel.

She had a decision to make.

Continue up the road and attempt to find Winter Lake Lodge and hope they had a room.

Or fight the fatigue pulling at her, do a U-turn, get back on the highway, and leave.

CHAPTER 3

8PM SUNDAY - WINTER LAKE, New York, USA

STONE PUSHED THE PEAK OF HIS BALL CAP UP AS HE leaned forward and gaped through the windshield. "Jesus."

If he didn't know better, he'd think he'd driven onto a movie set.

The town of Winter Lake looked picture-perfect, and he didn't know whether to be thankful the place was so tiny or curse the lack of anonymity a place this small would afford Sophie.

Chip had locked down her location through her rental car. Luckily for them, it had a GPS tracker fitted and they were able to pinpoint her exact whereabouts with ease. Of course, if *they* could, so could her stalker, George Henry Hagar.

Although Chip seemed to think the brains behind the

hack into Landlocked's system was the kid they'd hauled out of bed yesterday...or was it the day before? Damn time zones. He shook his head. Didn't matter. Right now he had to set eyes on Sophie.

He'd hit LA, cleared customs, and called Ford, only to be told to turn right back around and hop on another plane —ticket waiting for him at the counter—to New York. The state.

On arrival in Albany, he'd switched his phone on to find a message telling him a rental SUV was waiting, and to hightail it north to a place called Winter Lake.

His phone rang, vibrating against his hip where it was wedged in his pocket. Tapping the device wrapped around his right ear, Stone answered, "Yeah."

"Find her?" His boss wasn't one for pleasantries, especially on a job with an element of urgency, and getting to Sophie was definitely an immediate necessity.

"Just hit town," Stone responded. He eased off the gas to avoid rear-ending the car in front of him.

"You drive like an old lady," Ford growled. "I want eyes on her. Chip thinks he's found Hagar. The stupid asshole used a credit card to pay for a hotel room on the outskirts of Albany."

"When?" Stone had driven out of Albany about three hours earlier.

"Thirty minutes ago."

"So he's behind me?" That seemed unlikely. The guy had been on the same plane to LA as Sophie, while Stone had been a day behind. Surely he hadn't lost her? They couldn't be that lucky.

"Yeah, but I'm thinking he's either headed your way, or he's already been and gotten the lay of the land. All our research shows Winter Lake is a teeny-tiny blip on the map."

"If that," he muttered, while scanning the main street. One side was lined with a boardwalk and shops, the other what appeared to be a strip of parkland edging the lake he assumed the town got its name from. Not that you could see much of the park with all the tents and stalls and holy shit! A Ferris wheel!

"Our perp is going to want to get at Sophie without drawing attention, and he can't do that in a town like Winter Lake without a plan."

Stone agreed.

If *he* were doing the stalking, he'd scope out the place—and his target—retreat to a safe location to decide on his strategy, then return to execute the plan at a time when the least amount of people would be around.

Stone eyed the festival lining the lake's edge…or when the place was teaming with people.

Things were quiet now, most of the stalls were packed up or packing up for the night.

"Hey, can you get Chip to find out what's happening in Winter Lake at the moment?" Stone asked Ford.

"Why? What are you seeing?"

"Some kind of festival, I think," Stone answered.

"Let me…ah, here we go." Ford was quiet a moment, probably reading a report on the town. "It appears as though Ms. Collins has stumbled into the middle of the annual Ice Breaker Festival."

"Ice breaker?"

"Yep. Things started up this weekend and go all week, finishing up with the breaking of the ice and fireworks next weekend. Seems to draw in quite a crowd each year."

Great. Just great. Hagar could easily get lost in the crowd.

"Do we know how he's finding her?" Stone asked. "Chip said he wasn't on her flight out of LA, so he can't have tailed her here. Even if he caught a plane after hers using one of his aliases, he couldn't know where she stayed last night or where she headed this morning. Unless he *was* on her plane out of LA yesterday and we haven't figured out his new identity."

"Hmm... Hang on a sec." Ford put him on hold and Stone maneuvered the car around a truck parked half at the curb and half on the road.

He drove on, following the GPS instructions to Winter Lake Lodge, and waited for his boss to get back on the line while his instincts hummed, told him they were missing something.

"We've got a problem." Ford's voice boomed in his ear.

Stone's spine stiffened and his gut rolled with dread. "What?"

"Chip said the room charge was done over the net, so Hagar could be anywhere."

"Like here." It wasn't a question.

"Yep."

Fuck. "Did we get a good headshot of this prick yet?"

Stone needed a face. Until he knew exactly who he was looking for, everyone was a potential threat and so far the man had donned several different disguises from blond to black hair, blue to brown eyes; he was like a chameleon.

Add in Sophie's original vague description and they still weren't sure who they were looking for. And the kid hadn't been any help. According to Aiden he wasn't able to give the sketch artist anything that even looked like the man in the images they already had.

"I'll email the best ones we've got."

"Thanks."

"Don't thank me yet. Hagar's got a full beard in most and if he's smart, he's shaved that off or it's fake."

Stone hoped the bastard wasn't smart, except he'd proven smarter than any of them—or luckier. Stone couldn't decide which. "Whatever we've got will do." It would have to.

The Lodge came up on the right and he pulled into the driveway, maneuvering the big SUV around the curved gravel drive until he came to a parking lot. He swung into a spot beside a bright red convertible.

"Um, boss...please tell me Sophie isn't driving a damn sports car," Stone mumbled.

Ford chuckled. "Is it red?"

"*Fuck.*"

"Yep. Our girl doesn't know the first thing about flying under the radar."

Stone sighed. He didn't need her making his job more difficult. "How do you want me to play this?"

"She doesn't know you're coming because I can't reach her and neither can her manager. It appears she's been savvy enough to turn her phone off, even if she hasn't stopped using her credit card. But she does know we were hired to protect her and find this guy. You get to her, show her your security credentials, and get her to call her manager or me."

"Let's hope it's that easy." He wouldn't hold his breath.

"I met with her a couple of weeks ago when we took the job. She's not stupid but she's not used to hiding from crazies either. And don't forget we were all under the impression this guy was nothing more than an obsessed fan."

"He's obsessed all right," Stone replied.

"She'll work with you once she knows she can trust you," Ford assured him.

"I hope so. I'll check in after I make contact."

"Gotcha. Watch your back. Hagar's proven to be a wild card. I don't want to send anyone else in unless I absolutely have to. Jack followed you out there but he's going to hang back for now. I've got him heading to the hotel Hagar booked in Albany to check it out then he'll head your way."

"I want to know what he finds."

"Of course. Oh, and her manager doesn't want the press involved so at this point I'd rather play this close to the vest. If the local law gets called in, we might have a problem keeping things under wraps."

"No worries." He didn't want or need Jack or anyone else coming in and making things more complicated. The less attention they drew to Sophie, the better.

Ideally, Stone would like to lock her down somewhere while Jack hunted Hagar. Then they could neutralize the threat before it got anywhere near Sophie.

"Usual check-ins. I don't like this out-of-country, different-time-zone bullshit. I'd be far happier if the team was in one place."

"I've got this."

"I know." Ford's confidence in Stone's ability rang through in his voice and Stone smiled as he disconnected.

Pulling the Bluetooth from his ear, he reached behind the seat for his backpack. He checked his gear. He didn't like not having his gun on him but he didn't want to freak anyone out by wearing his shoulder holster.

This might be a country where hunting was common place, not to mention where guns were every citizen's right, but that didn't mean a guy visibly carrying a handgun wouldn't draw attention, and possibly the law.

Opening the door he stopped short.

The sultry voice of Sophie Collins floated on the air. Surrounded him. Although he couldn't see her from where he sat.

Hopping out, he locked the SUV and followed the sweet song until he found her at the back of the lodge on a patch of grass close to the lake.

Dusk's shadows shrouded her in an otherworldly glow, giving her and that siren's voice an ethereal quality.

It made him think of mermaids and sailors, the latter being lured to their deaths by the formers' seductive song.

For several moments, he stood immobile, mesmerized by the woman and the voice that had captivated millions. Anyone up on his or her pop music would recognize her in a heartbeat.

That thought got him moving. He swiftly scanned the

area and determined no one was around, although that didn't mean someone wasn't watching.

Wanting her out of sight, Stone strode forward. "Sophie."

Her voice cut off mid-word and she spun around, eyes wide, mouth open, long brown hair flying over her shoulders. Scrambling to her feet, she backed up a few steps before he realized she was about to run, stopping Stone dead in his tracks.

"I'm not going to hurt you." He held his hands open out by his sides. "I'm here to help. Your manager, Reginald Feldman, and my boss, Ford Moreland, have been trying to call you. My name is Stone. They sent me to protect you."

It was a lot of information for her to swallow in one go, but if he didn't get it out quickly he might have to chase her down, and that wasn't something he wanted to risk.

"I don't have my phone."

Relieved she hadn't bolted, Stone took an easy breath and the tension in his muscles dialed back a notch. "We can go inside to get it."

She shook her head. "I don't have it at all. I left it at home."

"In Sydney?"

She nodded.

Clever move or panicked rush? "That's okay, you can use mine. Or we can go inside and see if you can use the landline. Although I'd prefer you used mine. It's fitted with a blocker."

"A blocker?"

"It stops anyone from tracing the origin of the call if they've tagged your manager's phone."

"Oh. Right." She took a step towards him then stopped. "Do you have any ID on you?"

Stone smiled. At least she was smart enough to question him. Maybe keeping her safe wouldn't be a problem once she spoke to Ford.

"I'm going to take my wallet out of my back right-hand pocket and throw it to you. My driver's license is in there, along with credit cards and my Landlocked security ID. You can check the name matches on all of them."

"Okay."

He pulled his wallet out and easily tossed it the ten meters separating them.

She caught it left-handed and rapidly flicked through the various cards until she came to his security ID. Holding it up, she glanced between him and her hand several times.

Her lips twitched into a smile. "Okay, Mr. *Stone Mason*, pass me your phone."

CHAPTER 4

Sophie ended her second call in ten minutes and drew in a deep breath.

The first call had been to her manager; she'd spoken to Reginald only long enough for him to demand she call Ford Moreland and promise to do whatever the other man said.

It made sense. Mr. Moreland was an expert in the personal protection business, and it appeared as though his company also specialized in hunting down crazy stalkers, because he'd informed her they'd identified the man they believed was following her.

George Henry Hagar.

She'd never heard of him. Had no idea who he was or why he'd fixated on her.

And she couldn't be positive the man with the weird blue eyes she'd glimpsed in numerous places—including outside her house—in recent weeks was this George person, but it seemed likely.

She couldn't be unlucky enough to have two stalkers, could she?

"Everything okay?"

The deep rumbly voice jolted her out of her thoughts and she turned to look at the man standing next to her.

Stone Mason.

He wasn't at all what she imagined a personal body-guard would look like.

His brown hair was a little longer than the picture on his security ID, his face a touch boyish with a deep dimple in each cheek, and while he definitely had muscles, he didn't appear intimidating or menacing in a he-man, hired-muscle way.

Oh, she was positive Stone Mason could do his job. Mr. Moreland didn't strike her as the type to hire anyone who couldn't. She had no doubt the man in front of her had the ability to deal with the crazy one following her.

Problem was she struggled to move beyond how hand-some Stone was. He looked more like a movie star than the bodyguard protecting said movie star.

Not that his good looks meant he couldn't be protec-tive—or deadly. There was something understated about the threat he posed. He didn't appear threatening exactly, it was more a vibe he gave off, an aura that surrounded him.

Intuition told her he would put her in her place if she stepped out of it, and it was the way her insides tightened and warmed along with that instinct that had her a little off balance, that's all.

And she wasn't ready to figure out what the tremor

meant, the one that rattled her when their gazes connected.

She'd seen plenty of gorgeous men in her life. Being a celebrity guaranteed she was surrounded by some seriously yummy eye-candy a lot of the time.

Of course, the majority of those men were shallow, self-centered assholes, and none had inspired an instant attraction like the one she was experiencing with her new *personal* bodyguard.

It had been years since she'd had such a strong physical reaction to a man. If it wasn't for this whole stalker thing, she might be inclined to do something about it.

"Soph?"

"Huh?" She gave herself a mental slap and smiled. "Sorry. Yes. Everything is fine. Well no, not fine, but... bloody hell." She blew out a breath and his mouth curved up on one side, the dimple sinking deep, making her stomach flutter.

"What did Ford say?" he asked.

"That I should do whatever you tell me to do so you can keep me safe."

The other side of his mouth curled up. Dimple times two and *bam*, there was that fluttery sensation again. "And will you? Do whatever I say?"

She eyed him warily. There was something in his smile —the twinkle in his eyes—that made her think he didn't believe she would...and might enjoy it if she didn't.

An unexpected sexual jolt shot through her at the thought of him demanding her obedience.

Pushing her wayward thoughts aside, she concentrated

on the more important aspect of his appearance and asked, "Can you keep him away?"

In a flash, his expression turned serious and he took a step closer. Heat rolled off his body and brushed her bare skin. He leaned in and warm air fanned over her face, sending a shiver down her spine and a wave of goose bumps from her head to her toes.

"He'll have to go through me to get to you."

She believed him. Except...

"He got inside my house." The words were little more than a whisper as they slipped past her suddenly trembling lips, and she swallowed, her throat constricting with the burst of fear that exploded through her.

"I know."

Her vision blurred. "He was at the hotel in LA." Her nose tingled. *Bloody hell*. She wouldn't cry. She hadn't yet. She'd be damned if she would let the emotion spill out now.

"I promise you. He won't get past me." Had he moved closer?

"Okay." She blinked rapidly, though the action didn't stop a tear from escaping and sliding down her cheek.

"Soph." He reached out and cupped her face, his thumb sweeping the wetness from her skin. "I promise. I'll keep you safe."

"I don't understand. Why is this happening?" The fierce determination that had held her together for the last few days cracked. "W-what did I do?"

He pulled her into his arms and held her against his chest, tucking her head beneath his chin. "You didn't do anything. This guy is sick and if he hadn't zeroed in on you, he would have found someone else to fixate on."

"I—" A sob broke loose, the sound raw and sharp as it ripped out of her throat.

"Ssh…" He rubbed his large hands up and down her back, easing the chill inside her. "You're safe now."

She didn't need his reassuring words. For some inexplicable reason, the feel of his arms around her—the strength in his embrace—the warmth surrounding her, soaking into her, made her believe she'd not only be safe, but that she'd found the one place where she didn't have to pretend to be strong. Didn't have to do everything herself.

In Stone Mason's arms, she could let down her guard, let herself rely on someone else.

It was as unsettling as it was comforting and tempting.

Unable to resist the safety he represented, Sophie gave in to the need and let all the emotions she'd bottled up over the last few days free. She looped her arms around his waist and held on to fistfuls of his shirt as her walls broke wide open.

She didn't know how long it took before she calmed down, before she could take a breath without choking on it, but once she did and the dampness under her cheek registered, embarrassment flooded her.

She hadn't cried in front of anyone—never mind *on* a perfect stranger—in years.

With a sniffle, she tried to pull away. "I'm sorry."

"No. Don't." His arms tightened around her, held her against him. "Give yourself a minute."

She laughed, the sound broken by a hiccup. "I think I've had my minute."

"After the last few weeks, especially the last few days, you deserve more than one."

Did he have to be so sympathetic? If he didn't stop she'd start crying again. Leaning her head back, she sought his gaze with hers. "I—"

She wasn't ready for the tremor that shook her when her gaze connected with his. Whatever it was that sparked between them, it was potent. At least on her end.

"Sophie?"

She jerked in his arms and took a step back, except instead of letting her go, Stone smoothly slid one arm around her waist and kept her at his side. He managed to put her a little behind his body as they turned to face the woman who stood a few feet away.

"Is everything all right, Sophie?" Alice, the woman from the registration desk, asked, concern creasing her brow.

"Oh, yes, I…" God, how did she explain having a body-guard? Or the fact she'd just been bawling her eyes out all over him?

"Hi. I'm Stone." He extended his right hand. "Soph's boyfriend."

Boyfriend?

Her bodyguard-*boyfriend* disguised her shocked gasp by tugging her closer and hiding her face against his chest. He even dropped a kiss on the top of her head.

"Oh! How lovely." Alice stepped closer, shook Stone's hand. "Sophie didn't mention you'd be joining her."

"She didn't know I was coming. I got away at the last

minute and wanted it to be a surprise." He tipped his face down, his gaze finding Sophie's, and smiling, he winked. "That's why she was crying. Soph gets a little emotional sometimes."

"I'm Alice. Alice Dean. Welcome to Winter Lake Lodge."

"Nice to meet you," he said with a grin that showed those enthralling dimples. Poor Alice blushed from neck to forehead at the sight.

"Well, if you two will follow me, I'll show you to your room. As I told Sophie earlier, it's not the best but it'll do in a pinch. All our available rooms are booked because of the festival, so I've cleared up an attic room in the employees' wing that hasn't been used in a while. It has its own en suite; the plumbing might be ancient but it works." Alice, the blush still riding her cheeks, spun on her heel and led the way across the yard.

Sophie stood on her toes so she could whisper in Stone's ear. "Boyfriend?"

"No other way to stay close to you without revealing what's really going on."

"We don't need to stay in the same room."

He chuckled. "So is this you doing whatever I say?"

Bloody hell. He had her there.

Sighing, she dropped back on her heels and muttered, "Fine. C'mon, *boyfriend*, let's go see our room."

CHAPTER 5

STONE SAT on the end of the bed and watched Sophie pace.

She'd been doing it for twenty minutes now and while he didn't mind staring at her ass or the sexy swish of her skirt against the back of her thighs when she headed away from him, the muttering under her breath and the frown on her pretty face on the return trip were getting to him.

"Okay. Enough." He patted the bed next to him. "Sit down and talk to me."

"This isn't going to work. We can't stay in this room together." She stopped moving, hands on hips. "There's only one bed."

"It's a big bed…"

Keeping her distance, she glared at him. "I'm not sleeping with you."

He laughed. Sleeping was the last thing he wanted to do

with her in that bed, but he was disciplined and could control his base urges.

"Your virtue is safe. I'm not going to jump you, Soph."

Shaking her head, she muttered, "It's not *you* I'm worried about," and spun around to begin her trek across the room again.

He wasn't touching that comment with a ten-foot bargepole. He wasn't oblivious to the attraction arcing between them but he had no intention of acknowledging it. He had a job to do. One that required no distractions.

"I said I'd keep you safe, and I will."

Stone didn't take his vow to protect her lightly. He'd promised no one would get to her—and they wouldn't. His dedication to the job was one thing, but from the second he'd wrapped his arms around her, he'd developed a bone-deep need to see that nothing and no one hurt Sophie Collins.

The sentiment sat outside the parameters of his job. And it was a sensation he wasn't familiar with.

"I know." She sighed, stopped with her back to him. "But please tell me I'm not the only one feeling this."

Stone's insides churned. He could lie—to her and himself—or he could own up to there being something other than his commitment to do the job he was hired to do. "I'm here to do a job..."

"And that's it?" she demanded, spinning around; her gaze drilled him, dared him to lie.

He wasn't used to such candidness from a woman. Most of the females he'd encountered didn't deal in honesty, and they weren't direct like Sophie either. There always seemed to be some game they were playing, some sort of subterfuge going on.

It was refreshing to have things out in the open, and if he joined her in being honest, he had to admit her straight-forward approach turned him on. "No."

"What do we do about it?"

"Nothing."

She stared at him, her mouth open. "You can ignore it?"

God, he hoped so. If not, he could be putting her at risk. "I have to. Your safety comes before anything else."

"Right." She rolled her eyes. "So we just hang out in this room for hours and hours and sleep in the same bed and pretend we don't want to do anything remotely sexual to each other."

"Yep." His hands fisted. He could—*would*—keep his desires in check. Her life could depend on his ability to do his job, and the last thing he needed was a distraction. Even if it was the sexiest one he'd ever encountered.

"And how does that work when we leave the room and have to act as though we're a couple?"

Good question. Stone had no idea how they'd work that. "We'll hold hands?"

Sophie laughed. "I'm pretty sure someone as *emotional* as me would require more intimate PDA than that."

She was right. He wasn't even sure he could stop at holding her hand. If they hadn't been interrupted earlier, he'd have done more than hold her while she cried.

Which made him a selfish prick.

She'd been frightened and upset and all he could think about was how amazing she felt in his arms.

They needed to get off this subject before he said "fuck it" and pulled her into his arms again—and this time gave in to his desire to know how she tasted.

"When was the last time you slept?" he asked.

"What?" She frowned at him.

"Sleep. When did you last get some solid hours of sleep?" He needed to avoid the thing between them for now or he'd be finding out how she tasted in places other than her mouth. "You look worn out."

She grimaced. "Gee, thanks."

"I didn't mean you look bad." Quite the opposite. She looked good enough to eat. *Not going there.*

She smiled weakly. "It's okay. I get it." She sighed and said, "I got a couple of hours last night, maybe the same the night before."

"Why don't you have a shower and I'll see if I can find something to eat for dinner, then you can go to bed early. I'll sit in the chair by the door so you know you're safe."

"And when will *you* sleep?"

"I can sleep in snatches sitting up. And I'm a light sleeper, so if anyone tries to enter the room I'll be awake before they get through the door. Or window." Not that he thought anyone would climb in through the rooftop window, but it was still an entry point that needed protecting.

Plus he'd be awake all night anyway, with her in the bed a few feet away, but he wasn't about to admit that to her.

Glancing at the window then the door, she asked, "Do you think he'll come here?" She chewed her bottom lip and

Stone had to stop himself from walking over and tugging that plump flesh free. With his teeth.

"We think he's close. I won't lie to you about that. Or anything. I believe he's here in town, which is why I need you to tell me if you see him or feel like you're being watched. Anything that triggers your flight-or-fight instinct."

"Do you have a gun?"

The question took him off guard, although it shouldn't have. "Yes."

"Will you teach me how to shoot it?"

"No."

"But—"

"No. I'll teach you some self-defense moves. Tomorrow. After you get some rest. But you're not getting your hands on my gun."

"I want to be able to protect myself," she argued.

"That's what you have me for."

"And what about when you aren't with me?"

Stone rose to his feet. "Let's get one thing clear. The only time I won't be right by your side, with my eyes on you, is when you use the bathroom—and I'll walk you in and check the room before standing outside the door, so you'll never be without my protection."

"Oh."

He moved closer, watched a shiver rock her body, her eyes widen as he got closer. "Soph."

"Yes." She licked her lips.

"I'm not letting anything happen to you."

"Because it's your job."

"Yes." He lifted a hand, tucking a thick strand of wavy hair behind her ear. "And because I can't bear the thought of anything happening to you."

"We just met."

He smiled. "Yeah. Doesn't seem to matter."

"Is this normal? When you guard someone?"

Stone shook his head. "Never before you."

"I—"

"We need to hold that thought, Soph. I can't do my job if my head isn't in the right place. I need you to help me out here."

"I don't want to."

She pouted, and for the first time her age entered his mind. "How old are you?"

Her chin jutted out, her eyes narrowed. "I'm legal."

He laughed. "I know that. How legal?"

"Twenty-five."

Seven years. Not a huge gap... Why was he even thinking about their age difference?

She was a job. He had to remember that. For now.

"Grab what you need and take a shower. I'll go down and see if I can beg, borrow, or steal food from somewhere."

"I thought you weren't going to leave me alone."

"You'll be locked in the bathroom, with the room locked as well. There's only one way up here, through the employees' kitchen, which means anyone who tried to get to you would have to come past me. Regardless, don't open the bedroom door to anyone. Not even me. I'll take the key."

Sophie gave him a brief nod then went to her bag in the corner. Stone waited while she pulled out clothes and a small toiletries bag. He kept his eyes averted in an effort to not glimpse anything he might obsess over.

Like her underwear.

The last thing he needed to think about was what lay beneath her clothes.

On her way to the en suite tucked into the corner of the room, she shot him a small smile, and he held his breath until the door closed between them and the lock clicked into place. Now that there was a solid piece of timber separating them, he could let himself relax.

His muscles ached with the release of tension. He hadn't realized how tight he'd held himself. He'd never had to control his emotions the way he had in the last hour. His birth name might be Stone, but he was also a stone by nature. Nothing got to him. No situation. No person.

Until now.

Sophie Collins—with her mass of wavy brown hair, slender curves, and brutally honest green eyes—had slid right beneath his skin. For the life of him, Stone couldn't work out how or when.

If he couldn't lock down his wayward libido, they'd be in for a world of trouble. But he wasn't fooling himself. It wasn't only his hormones that were interested in Sophie. And that right there was the crux of his problem.

Under any other circumstances, he'd be all over the pretty singer. She wasn't his type and yet bare minutes in her presence and he wanted more. Except these weren't different circumstances, and they were anything but normal, *and* he had a job to do.

Keep Sophie safe.

Find the fucker stalking her.

Deliver her home unharmed.

The question was, could he do his job without the chemistry between them getting in the way...and would he walk away when the job was over?

CHAPTER 6

Sophie kept glancing over her shoulder expecting Stone to come charging down the stairs into the kitchen and drag her back to their room.

Breathing a sigh of relief when she found the stairwell behind her empty she turned back to the woman who'd been talking non-stop since Sophie had ventured downstairs for a glass of water a few minutes ago.

"Everything all right?" Alice asked with a frown.

"Oh. Yes." She smiled. "Sorry. Just a little distracted."

With a knowing smile, Alice nodded. "I can understand that. You should talk that man of yours into taking you to the Ice Breaker Festival tonight for the dance auction." The older woman slid a tray of yummy-looking chocolate chip cookies into the oven.

Sophie would love one of those cookies. She'd also love to get out and see some of Winter Lake. Stone had banned her from leaving the room though; leaving the *Lodge* would definitely be out of the question, but she couldn't tell Alice that. "Dance auction?"

"People auction themselves off for dances to raise money for town projects. This year the proceeds are going toward the high school. The sports department is in sore need of new equipment," Alice explained.

"Sounds like a good cause and my kind of fun." And it did. Well, anything except looking at the walls of her room would be fun right now. Especially when she was supposed to keep her mind—and hands—off Stone.

"What sounds like your kind of fun?" Heat touched her back a split-second before Stone's arm slid around her shoulders banding across the top of her chest, his hard body pressing against her spine.

The man hadn't made a sound coming down the stairs or walking up behind her.

"I was telling Sophie about tonight's dance auction. You should go and enjoy a drink and a twirl. See some of what Winter Lake has to offer other than your room." Alice winked at them. "Not that there's anything wrong with the rooms here at the Lodge." Her smile turned into a frown. "Well, most of them. I'm sorry I couldn't offer you a better room."

"It's—"

"Where's the auction?" Stone asked as he tightened his hold and pulled her closer.

Sophie shivered as warm air ruffled the loose strands of hair near her temple. He seemed to surround her with heat. Just when she'd managed to cool her libido he ramped it back up again.

"It's in front of the gazebo in Lake Front Park, right in the middle of town. I'll be heading down there as soon as these cookies finish baking." Alice loaded the empty mixing bowl into the dishwasher. "I can't wait to pop on my dancing shoes and take a spin around the floor."

"Maybe we'll go check it out." Stone lowered his face beside Sophie's and spoke into her ear. "You left the room without me."

To Alice his words would sound innocent, but Sophie heard the underlying accusation.

"I only came down to get a drink."

Which was true. She'd had no intention of leaving the building, and wouldn't have stayed in the kitchen for as long as she had if Alice hadn't been there and started talking to her. She didn't want to be rude.

Lowering his voice further, so only she could hear, he whispered, "Don't do it again or I'll tie you to the bed."

A shudder worked its way down her spine, leaving heat and tingles behind. "Oh."

"You like that idea?" His lips brushed the shell of her ear. "Jesus, Soph, don't tempt me," he growled.

"I—"

"Let's go." Stone spun her out of his arms and around to face him.

"Where?"

"The auction."

"We're going out?"

"Safer than staying in at this point." He grabbed her hand and wove their fingers together. "We'll see you there, Alice."

"Have fun."

Sophie barely had time to glance over her shoulder at a smiling Alice because Stone tugged her behind him so fast, she had to jog or fall on her face.

"We're really going out?" Sophie asked as he towed her through the rear door of the employees' wing.

"Yep." He marched them through the grounds to the parking lot in front of the lodge and right up to his car where he flung the door open and ordered, "Get in."

She obeyed but only because she was desperate to get out of their room and find a distraction from the attractive man she shared it with.

After a near sleepless night, today had been an exercise in torture. He'd insisted on showing her some self-defense moves, which meant he put his hands on her.

Big, strong, capable hands.

All. Over. Her.

Hands she'd fantasized about touching her in completely inappropriate ways, considering he was her bodyguard and they'd just met.

Stone wasted no time getting them moving once she'd climbed into the passenger seat. He jogged around to the driver's side and had the SUV started and reversing out of its spot before either of them had buckled their seat belts.

"Where's the fire?" she asked with a chuckle.

"In my fucking pants," he growled through clenched teeth.

Oh my. What could she say to that?

"I've got rules."

"Rules?" she squeaked.

"Don't leave my side. Not for anything. If you have to use the bathroom, I'll go with you. Don't take a drink from anyone but me. No *dancing* with anyone but me."

"I don't dance."

"What?" He glanced at her briefly.

"I won't be dancing." She wasn't about to tell him why.

"Might be for the best anyway."

His cryptic comment made perfect sense to her. Being held in his arms was dangerous. They'd learned that earlier, when he'd shown her how to get away if someone grabbed her from the front and they'd ended up on the floor, Sophie spread out beneath him.

He certainly lived up to his name. The man was hard as stone. Every. Inch.

Their tumble was the reason he'd taken a shower. A cold one.

Sophie smiled.

At least she wasn't alone in her sexual frustration. She wasn't used to denying herself. She wasn't a diva who threw her weight around to get what she wanted, but when it came to men, she'd always been open and honest about what she wanted and what she didn't.

And she wanted Stone.

Badly.

This denying-their-attraction was bullshit. But he'd made it clear. She was a job.

"We're here." He switched the car off. "Wait 'til I come around and get you."

Sophie didn't get a chance to agree or disagree. He was

out of the car, striding around the front, his eyes scanning the area, in less time than it took to blink.

Instead of stepping back and offering a hand to help her out, he opened the door and moved into the gap, putting his face right in hers. "Rules."

"Rules?"

"What are they? If you can't tell me, we're not going any farther."

"Um, don't leave you."

"More than arm's length is too far. If I have to lean over, or worse, take a step, we're out of here. What else?"

"Don't take a drink from anyone but you."

"And?"

"No dancing unless you're my partner."

He patted her thigh. "Good girl."

Sophie shivered, a thrill of delight at his praise—his touch—streaked through her and detonated low in her belly.

"I mean it, Soph, those are not negotiable."

"I know." She didn't need him to tell her that. It was written all over his face, in his stance. He vibrated with tension, and while she found it sexy as hell that he was all macho-alpha, she knew he was only being that way to keep her safe.

And just like that, hormones took a backseat to fear.

Glancing around, she searched for the eyes that had haunted her sleep.

Stone's hand gripped her chin and turned her back so she had no choice but to focus on him.

"He won't get to you through me. Trust me. Letting him get his hands on you is the last thing I'm going to do."

"Because it's your job."

His gaze probed hers. "It *is* my job."

Sophie sucked in a breath. "But that's not all…"

"No. That's not the only reason he's not getting his hands on you."

He didn't say anything else, just stared at her as though trying to telepathically transmit some kind of message. She wanted to ask him to elaborate. But she bit her lip to keep the questions burning her tongue from spilling out.

Now wasn't the time.

After what seemed like forever, Stone took a deep breath. "C'mon, before I change my mind and take you back to the lodge." He tangled his fingers through hers and helped her step out of the SUV.

Slinging an arm around her shoulders, Stone swiftly ushered her across the dark parking lot and onto the main street. A variety of stalls lined the blocked off road.

People chatted in groups, wandered between booths, drinks and food in their hands, and kids of all ages ran around, weaved through legs, laughing and shouting.

The closer they got to the center of town the louder the music grew.

Alcohol and fried food aromas filled the air and numerous flickering torches set up along the park's edge, both by the street and at the lake shore, illuminated hundreds of people.

There were small bonfires in a long line along the edge of the lake too and Sophie took it all in.

She grinned. She needed this. Needed to get out, be one of the crowd, feel music thrumming through her. Absorb the energy from a large group of people having a good time.

It had been ages since her last live show. She missed it. She loved working on her songs, loved laying them down in the studio, getting them just right, but in spite of the nerves that plagued her before she stepped on stage, it was singing in front of an audience that Sophie really lived for.

And while she wouldn't be on stage tonight, would not be performing for this clearly up-for-a-good-time crowd, just being among them would help relieve some of her tension, take her mind off the reason she was really here.

For tonight, she'd be just an everyday woman out with a handsome man.

CHAPTER 7

STONE HELD Soph in front of him, his arms circling her
waist, and watched the auction—the crowd surrounding
them.

They'd found a spot off to the side of the makeshift
dance floor, out of the way, where no one seemed to take
any notice of them. He wanted to keep it that way, and not
only because she needed to keep a low profile.

No. Stone wasn't going to hide from the fact he wanted
her all to himself.

It was the reason he'd decided to risk bringing her out
tonight. If they'd stayed in their room a minute longer, he'd
have lost the battle against his libido and taken her.

Instead, he'd taken a cold shower, and she'd skipped out
of the room, giving him a heart attack when he'd discovered her gone.

That moment right there. The razor-sharp slice of

terror that slashed through him, almost took him to his knees.

Definitely not his usual work-mode reaction. Nowhere in sight was the stone-cold professional he'd been in the past. Nope. This Stone felt like he'd been gutted.

With a blunt letter opener.

He pulled Soph in a little tighter just to remind himself that he hadn't lost her.

She fit so perfectly in his arms, with her head resting on his shoulder, that Stone knew his control was history.

Hell, maybe it had been from the second he'd touched her yesterday.

There was no way he could walk away from this woman after they dealt with her stalker. But until then, he needed to keep a clear head, and fighting his attraction to her wasn't giving him that—so maybe he should accept it, stop struggling against their chemistry and enjoy this unexpected connection.

He wouldn't take it far, but he wouldn't deny himself the opportunity to touch her, hold her. Possibly steal a kiss or two.

His body tightened, his jeans growing a little more uncomfortable at the thought of tasting her. Stone shifted his feet to keep from pressing his erection into her back.

The hard-on wasn't a new development. He'd sported some level of hardness since he'd first put his hands on her.

Damn awkward, and certainly not conducive to doing his job with a clear head. He needed to nix the thoughts of getting Soph naked until they were somewhere less public though.

Somewhere he knew her stalker couldn't get to her.

He scanned the crowd around them, looking for anyone who might be a threat. None of the pictures Ford had emailed him had been clear, and with various hair colors and lengths, and the facial hair Hagar had, there was no way Stone could get a good idea of his bone structure.

And Soph wasn't any help; the only clear thing she could tell them about the guy she'd seen was that he had ice blue, almost clear eyes, which meant he was still working blind.

They'd gotten nothing at the hotel in Albany either. There had been no sign Hagar had ever set foot in the place. They were hitting dead ends every direction they went.

From across the dance floor Jack caught his eye and subtly lifted his beer in acknowledgement. His Landlocked colleague had rolled into town earlier this afternoon. Stone didn't know where he was staying, and didn't care as long as Jack was close at hand.

While he hadn't wanted anyone else here, he had to admit he was relieved to know he had backup.

The auctioneer's voice boomed through the speakers set up throughout the park, announcing the final candidate on the auction block, dragging Stone's gaze back to the gazebo.

The guy who stood at the top of the pavilion stairs doing some kind of pose much to the amusement of the crowd looked like a lumberjack with his work boots, jeans, and flannel shirt; he quickly sold for a respectable hundred and fifty dollars.

Declaring the night a success, the auctioneer revealed the grand total of three and a half thousand raised. One thousand of that had come in for a woman named Covington.

The crowd had hooted and hollered when the man who'd made the only bid jumped up on stage decked out in full firefighting attire, tossed a check at the auctioneer, then tossed the leggy blonde over his shoulder as though he were rescuing her from a fire and made off with her.

Soph shifted against him and Stone couldn't resist dipping his head and nuzzling the hair behind her ear. He'd managed to keep himself in check so far. He might have wanted to drag her farther into the dark and do some scandalous things, considering their location, but he hadn't.

She tilted her head, moving into his touch, and Stone smiled. Her hands covered his, their fingers weaving together where they rested on her belly. He felt her moan more than heard it and his hips bucked forward, his cock thickening with the hot throb of his blood.

"Soph," he murmured in her ear.

"Please." She ground her ass against his groin.

"Fuck."

"Yes. Please."

Stone buried his face in the side of her neck and sucked in a breath.

Her scent filled him—invaded him—and if he opened his mouth he'd be able to see if she tasted as sweet as she smelled. He held back though. He didn't want them to go any further.

Not here.

A little suggestive movement to the music would be acceptable but keeping her in the dark away from prying eyes was bound to get them into trouble.

Reluctantly, he cupped her shoulders and pushed her forward. "Let's dance."

She looked over her shoulder, blinked. "What?"

"Dance. C'mon." He grabbed her hand and started for the dance floor but she dug in her heels and pulled him back. Glancing at her, he asked, "You don't want to dance?"

Soph looked past him at the dance area, her expression apprehensive. "I can't."

He tugged her closer. "It'll be fine. We'll keep to this side of the floor. It's shadowed, and with how crowded it is, no one will see you."

She shook her head. "No. I *can't*."

Studying her closely, he tried to determine what the problem was. If it wasn't fear of her stalker finding her then what—

A thought struck him. "What do you mean *can't*?"

A deep sigh raised and lowered her chest and a frown tipped the corners of her mouth down. She stepped into him, went to her toes, and whispered in his ear, "I've got two left feet. Actually, it's more like fifty."

Stone stared at her when she plopped back down on her heels. "But...you sing."

She laughed. "One thing has nothing to do with the other."

"But..." He shook his head and tried to get his mind around what she was saying. "*You sing*."

"Obviously all the musical talent is in my vocal cords,

because the second I try to move to music, I'm a danger to myself and those around me."

"I don't understand."

She sent him a sympathetic smile. "You and every dance instructor in Australia."

"You really can't dance?" It seemed inconceivable.

"Nope."

"But it's not that hard." Hell, if he could do it, anyone could.

"It is for me."

Stone looked over his shoulder at all the couples moving to the slow number currently playing. Focusing back on Soph, he said, "You don't really have to move, not to this song. I'll just hold you and we'll sway. I'll lead, you follow." Confident it would work, he tugged on her hand.

"I don't think—"

"No thinking, that's probably where you're going wrong."

"Going wrong?" She arched one eyebrow at him. "Really?"

"Maybe that was the wrong choice of words. C'mon, it can't be that bad."

With a tip of her head, she pursed her lips and eyed him for a moment. "Fine. It's your toes."

Soph let him lead her onto the floor and pull her into his arms. He held her close, kept his feet planted and rocked to the music. They swayed together, her body pressed along the length of his, and he couldn't stop himself from pulling her closer.

A second later she stepped on his left foot—then the

right one as she tried to get off the left one. Half a minute after that her knee bumped his before once again her foot came down on his as she attempted to move to the song. At the minute mark, her elbow connected with his ribs —*twice*.

His toes took another hit and she huffed out a breath. "Told you I was dangerous," she muttered.

He chuckled. "The injuries aren't life-threatening."

"Not yet. Give me a few more minutes. The song isn't over yet."

They lasted through the first song and a few words into the next before she lifted her head and smashed the top of it into his chin. Her hand came up and he had to duck to the side to avoid an index finger to the eye.

She grimaced as she rubbed the back of her head. "You still want to do this?" she asked.

He grinned, his arms still around her, their bodies still swaying. "Aren't you having fun?"

Staring at him wide-eyed, she asked, "Are *you*?"

Smiling, he dropped a kiss on the tip of her nose. "Every second with you is fun."

She laughed. "Is that what you call what we've been doing?"

"What would you call it?"

"Torture?"

"*Not* touching you is torture. This is pure pleasure in spite of your unruly limbs." He softened his words with a smile and lowered his head. With his mouth millimeters from hers, he said, "And this is pleasure so sweet, I'm not able to deny myself any longer."

He slanted his lips over hers and took her mouth.

She parted for him instantly, her tongue tangling with his as though they'd kissed a million times before and knew exactly how to get what they wanted, what they needed.

Tightening his arms, he snapped her closer, her breasts pressing into his chest, the tips hardening, as their kiss went deeper.

Heat flashed through him, consumed all caution in a blaze so scorching, he thought he might burst into flames.

His pants really did feel as though they were on fire now.

She pushed to her toes when he cupped her ass, their bodies lining up in all the best ways and Stone struggled to remember why he'd kept his hands off this woman. Why he couldn't take her here and now.

She broke her mouth away from his. Panted through parted lips as she stared at him with dilated eyes and flushed cheeks. "Bloody hell. We need to leave. Now."

"Agreed."

He spun her around and put his hands on her hips, steering her off the dance floor and toward the street.

They were almost to the sidewalk when she jerked to a stop and stepped back into him.

"What?" he asked, trying to see past her to what had brought a halt to their progress.

"I..." Her gaze searched the people moving around them. She shook her head. "Nothing. Sorry. Let's get out of here."

"Soph?"

"No. It's fine. C'mon."

Stone let her lead the way to the parking lot and his SUV while he scanned the area looking for any kind of threat.

Reaching the car he unlocked her door and helped her in. "Soph."

She turned his way and smiled. "Don't you dare back down now."

"I wasn't going to." He leaned into her. "But you need to be sure."

"I'm sure."

"I won't stop once I start."

"And yet here you are, stopping." She smiled and dragged a fingertip down his chest, hooked it in the top of his pants, and yanked. "Take me back to our room, Stone."

CHAPTER 8

"Soph."

Her name left Stone's lips like a prayer and a shiver raced through her as the whisper of sound vibrated over her skin, his warm breath tickling across her cheek.

His lips moved against hers and her eyelids fluttered closed, her body arching, her head dropping back, a moan of pleasure caught in her throat.

The man knew how to kiss, but his hands...god, his hands.

They swept up her sides, his thumbs grazing the bottom swells of her breasts, and she bowed toward his touch, urging him to move higher. Wanting him to touch her without her clothes between them.

"Soph..." He murmured her name once more, against the curve of her jaw this time. "You taste so sweet here. I need to find out if you taste the same all over."

She hummed in approval. If he wanted to move that

talented mouth all over her body, she wasn't going to stop him.

In fact...she'd give him a hand—or two.

Tangling her fingers in his hair, she tugged downward, directing him lower, until he took the hint and trailed his lips down her throat and across her chest.

"We need to get rid of these clothes." He pulled at the collar of her shirt, dragging it out of his way. "I want to see all of you."

"Yes." Opening her eyes, her gaze met his heated stare and that tremor she was growing accustomed to vibrated through her.

"Every single inch of you, Soph."

"Hmm..." He'd drugged her with his kisses. Made her dizzy with his caresses. "Okay."

He smiled. "So this is where you agree to do everything I say."

She bit her lip and nodded.

Smile growing bigger, he murmured, "Well then." He shoved her shirt up her torso. "Let's get you naked."

He pushed her top higher and she raised her arms to help him.

Clear of the first barrier between them, she reached for his shirt. "You too."

"Of course."

In a quick yank, Stone had the t-shirt over his head and tossed on the floor behind him.

He grinned. "Your turn."

She chuckled. "Is that how this works? We're taking turns?"

"Mmmm…" His lust-filled gaze caressed her breasts where they swelled at the top of her bra. "I think you've got more clothing on than me, so you should take off two pieces to every one of mine to make it fair."

Sophie studied him. He'd kicked off his shoes when they'd entered the room and with his shirt gone, it left four pieces by her count—jeans, underwear, and socks. She had five remaining—bra, jeans, panties and shoes. "I'm only one ahead of you."

"Two."

Before she could argue, Stone popped the button on his jeans, yanked down the zipper, and shoved them over his hips. Bending, he lifted each foot in turn and slipped free of his pants, taking his socks at the same time. He straightened and kicked the clothes aside.

"Five," he said with a smirk.

"You're…" She licked her lips, her gaze glued to the large erection pointing right at her. "*Commando?*" The word came out high-pitched, as though her vocal cords were being strangled, and sounded nothing like the high notes she occasionally hit in her songs.

"Always." He shrugged. "Makes for less laundry. Easier traveling."

"Oh." Her breath stuttered, her pulse raced. She wanted to touch him. Wanted to wrap her hand around his shaft and feel the heat and strength beneath the flushed skin. "Can I…" She reached out.

Stone emitted a choked growl when she gripped him.

He was hot and silky-soft against her fingers, and she couldn't resist sliding her hand up and down his hard length. Squeezing tighter on the up stroke, twisting a little on the down.

"Soph," he rasped, the gravelly tone of his voice spurring her on.

"I want to…" Giving in to the impulse, she dropped to her knees, bent her head, and sucked him between her lips.

His body jolted, hips bucking, and more of his flesh filled her mouth. "God. Soph. *Fuck.*"

She hummed and bobbed. Lashed with her tongue and sucked. She couldn't get enough of him, couldn't fit as much as she wanted in her mouth.

The taste of him, masculine and hot, his earthy scent, and his garbled sounds of pleasure made her mouth water, the extra saliva aiding the slide of her lips.

His hands found her head, his fingers tangling in her hair, pulling tight, but he didn't force her to move a certain way or go faster. It was as though he was holding on, as though he couldn't remain on his feet without that simple connection.

She gripped the base of his cock with her left hand, cupped and rolled and squeezed his balls with her right, all while sucking him deep, deeper, until his cock head hit her throat.

When she swallowed around the spongy tip, his shaft pulsed on her tongue and his fingers dug into her scalp, delivering a sharp surge of erotic pain.

"Fuck. Soph," he panted. "I'm close."

It never entered her mind to pull away, to finish him with her hands. She didn't think about anything except giving him the ultimate pleasure.

Hollowing her cheeks, she sucked harder and rolled his balls on her palm, gripping and tugging.

His hips bucked, his length throbbing and hardening on her tongue, and his grip on her head tightened, this time holding her still—taking control.

Keeping the rhythm and depth she'd set, he drove his shaft in and out for a few more strokes before he plunged deep and stiffened.

Warm fluid filled her throat and mouth. Swallowing fast, she sucked down every drop he gave her.

She'd never done it before. Never taken a man to his release with her mouth. Never wanted to.

"Jesus. Fuck." Stone's legs shook, his fingers on her head loosening. "What was that?"

Sophie licked up the last of his come as he pulled from her mouth. "A blow job?"

"No. That wasn't a blow job. Fuck, woman." He sank to his knees in front of her, cradled her face in his hands. "I've had blow jobs. But they were never like that. I think you blew the top of my head off."

The stab of jealousy that hit her at the thought of some faceless woman giving him pleasure was instantly soothed by his praise of her efforts. "I've never done that before."

"*What?*" He stared at her, eyebrows high on his brow. "You haven't sucked a cock?"

She laughed. "No. I've done that. I haven't..." Heat filled her face. "You know."

"Swallowed?" He smiled, his thumbs tracing along her lips. "Thank you."

Sophie smiled. "It doesn't seem right to say 'you're welcome', but, well, you're welcome."

Stone cupped her jaw tighter and, leaning in, kissed her.

Losing herself in the brush of his lips, the stroke of his tongue, she didn't notice him reach around and unhook her bra until the fabric gave way, her breasts spilling free, and the straps slipped from her shoulders.

"I think someone still has too many clothes on," he murmured against her mouth.

She drew in a breath. "We should do something about that."

"Yes, we should."

Without any effort at all, Stone hauled her into his arms and stood. He strode to the bed and gently placed her across it.

Eyes on hers, he slid the button on her jeans free and lowered the zipper. Tucking his fingers into the waistband at her hips, he dragged the denim down, hooking her underwear as he went.

When he reached her feet, he slipped off her ankle boots and tossed them aside; her pants and underwear quickly followed.

Grinning, he said, "Now we're even."

Expecting him to crawl up the bed, Sophie was surprised when he dropped to his knees on the floor and ran his hands up her shins, over her knees and up between her legs. Splaying his fingers on her thighs, he pushed them apart.

"You're so gorgeous, I don't know where to start."

Anywhere. Just keep touching me.

CHAPTER 9

STONE GRINNED and crawled onto the bed, caging Soph with his body. "Anywhere?"

Her eyes widened, her lips parting on a rush of air.

He chuckled. "Didn't mean to say that out loud, huh?"

She shook her head as color rose up her chest into her neck and flooded her face.

"I think it's safe to say I'll be touching you everywhere before I'm done with you."

His gaze snagged on her mouth when her tongue peeked out and slid over her bottom lip. The plump red flesh glistened and Stone couldn't resist following the path her tongue had taken with his own.

Dipping his head, he kept his eyes locked on hers and mirrored her move. Her eyes dilated and warm breath feathered over his lips. He inhaled, drew in her breath, pulled it deep to take that small part of her inside him—to claim it, *and* her, even if it was only that tiny bit.

They breathed the same air as he dragged his tongue back and forth across her mouth. He touched only her lips but every inch of him vibrated with the need to touch more. All of her.

Slow and thorough had been his plan, except now that they were naked, Soph beneath him, Stone couldn't remember why he'd thought that was a good idea. Couldn't remember what had taken so long to get here. He felt as though he'd waited to have her this way forever.

She's a job.

He ignored the voice of reason. It might be his job to keep her safe, but this—their mouths touching, their breaths mingling, their bare bodies inches apart—had nothing to do with his job and everything to do with a bone-deep need he could no longer deny.

Slowly, Stone lowered his body over hers. Her skin was soft and smooth against him and the hot cradle of her pussy pressed along his shaft, his balls slipping into the valley between her thighs when they opened.

They moaned in unison, the pleasure-filled sounds echoing around them and delivering a jolt of lust to his already-throbbing groin.

"Soph." He trailed his lips along her jaw to her ear. "I need you."

"Yes." She parted her legs wider and his cock sank deeper into the groove of her sex.

He needed to get a condom before the slick heat of her channel pulled him in and he took her without protection.

"Condom." Shaking with want, he rolled off her.

How he was ready to blow his load again was beyond him. He hadn't rebounded this quickly in years.

Couldn't remember the last woman he'd been with who'd inspired this level of lust.

Standing beside the bed, he grabbed his pants and searched the pockets for his wallet.

Digging through the sections of his wallet, he found a condom. Hastily tearing the packet open, he sheathed his straining cock with trembling fingers.

God, she had him on the edge, and she'd already blown his mind using her mouth. What the hell would happen when he got inside her?

With no more patience, he climbed back onto the bed and lay over her once more. "I'm sorry. I can't take my time. Can't be gentle."

"I don't want slow or gentle." Her hands found his head, her fingers grabbing his hair with a grip that would hurt if he wasn't so aroused he could barely see straight. "I want you to fuck me, Stone."

He'd never found a dirty mouth on a woman sexy, and maybe it was just Soph, but hearing her say the word "fuck", hearing her telling him to fuck her in that sultry voice...

He shifted his hips to the side and trailed a hand down her torso, across her belly and over her mound, until he slid his fingers into her wet folds. She was hot and slippery, her flesh soft and pliant beneath his touch.

"So wet," he murmured, before he took her mouth and drove his tongue inside at the same time as he thrust two fingers into her pussy.

She arched off the bed, her mouth pulling from his as a cry of pleasure burst from her throat.

Heat and moisture flooded her channel, coated his skin, and Stone found her clit with his thumb, adding pressured strokes to the sensitive bundle of nerves while driving his fingers in and out of her clenching body.

He wanted to taste her. Needed to taste her. And he would. Later. Right now he needed to be inside her more—required it—and he couldn't go there until he had her on the edge because the second he sank his cock into the slick, clinging walls of her pussy, he knew he'd lose his mind.

Lose all rational thought and consideration.

Her breasts heaved with each short breath and he bent his head to take one tantalizing peak between his teeth. Holding tight, he lashed the taut tip with his tongue several times before sucking the bud deep into his mouth.

Moaning, she moved into his touch, rocked her hips against his hand, and pressed her breast into his face, her hands wrapped around his head, keeping him in place.

She wiggled and bucked, and Stone loved that she wasn't afraid to take what she wanted from him.

One hand left his head and skated down his chest, over his abs, and finally to the thick shaft that felt as though it threatened to burst out of the latex surrounding it.

Like before, Soph showed no signs of shyness, curling her fingers around his length, stroking and squeezing until his eyes rolled back in his head.

"Soph." Not willing to give up her nipple, he spoke around it. "Too close."

She tugged on his cock. Squeezed. "Then fuck me already," she demanded.

Stone's balls contracted and made premature ejaculation a very real possibility for the first time in his life. "Fuck," he growled as he let go of her nipple.

"Yes." She squeezed him again—harder. "Fuck me."

God. She was going to kill him. Blood roared in his ears. Pounded in his veins—in his groin. Every part of him seemed to be one giant pulsing nerve ready to detonate at any second.

He had to get inside her. He'd put it off too long and ran the risk of filling the condom with the first slide into her heated flesh.

Removing his hand from between her legs, Stone gripped her hips and rolled to his back. "On top."

Soph quickly got on board with his plan and rose to her knees, her thighs straddling his hips. With that torturous hand, she held his cock and, lining the head up with her body, sank down over him.

Hot and plush, her pussy swallowed his entire length in one smooth glide. From tip to root, Stone's cock was surrounded by the wet clench of her body.

His balls tightened, his shaft throbbed, and it took all his strength to keep from thrusting up and driving his aching cock deeper.

He let her set the pace, palmed her hips, and guided her movements as she found a rhythm that tore at his restraint.

Steady and slow, Soph rode him with more enthusiasm

than skill but the tempo kept him from hurtling over the edge.

Stretching his thumb toward her center, he found her clit and pressed in a circular motion that soon had her breathing harder and moving faster.

It wasn't the driving beat his body craved but until he pushed her to the limit, he wouldn't take what he needed.

Without warning she gasped, her body jolting, her stride breaking. In the next moment her pussy clamped down on his cock in a punishing grip that threatened to unman him as her orgasm ripped through her—through *him*.

Grabbing her waist, Stone flipped them over, pulled her legs around his hips and pounded into her.

Hard and fast and deep, he plunged into her clenching pussy over and over and over. And when he thought he couldn't take any more, thought he'd go insane if he didn't find release, his body snapped.

Pulse after pulse of pleasure so extreme it hurt thumped through him. Scraped his bones and rattled his teeth. Burying his face into the curve of her neck, Stone thrust deep and held.

Panting and sweating and coming apart at the seams, he acknowledged the magnitude of the moment.

He'd had sex with Sophie Collins.

His client.

Fuck. He'd slept with his client.

Lifting off her, he slipped from her body and turned away. "Need to ditch the condom."

What he needed was a minute. A few seconds to regroup and process.

Ducking into the bathroom, he trashed the used latex and washed up. Should he get a warm cloth for Soph? He glanced up and his gaze collided with hers in the mirror.

"I have to use..." She waved her hand at the toilet.

"Oh. Right. Sure." Still a little—okay, a lot—off-kilter, Stone stepped out of the way to let her pass, then slipped out of the door. It closed with a soft click behind him. He ran a hand through his hair and muttered, "Shit."

What did he do now? Get dressed? Climb under the covers? He couldn't—shouldn't—fuck her again.

Not that she was just a fuck. He'd had plenty of those, and he knew what they'd done couldn't be called a fuck.

He didn't want to put a name to it though. Couldn't afford to.

His pants vibrated, drawing his attention away from his scattered thoughts. Reaching down, he scooped his jeans up and yanked the phone from his pocket.

Jack.

Dreading the coming conversation, Stone knew if he didn't answer this call, he'd find Jack at the door in minutes. He was lucky Jack wasn't banging on the door already.

Hitting accept, Stone brought the device to his ear. "Hey."

"What the hell, man?" Jack growled in his ear. "You kissed her!"

Fuck. He couldn't ignore or brush this aside. "We're pretending to be a couple."

"Bullshit. There was nothing pretend about that kiss. You all but devoured each other. I felt the heat clear across the dance floor."

"It was nothing." He needed to downplay it, or else Jack would tell Ford, and Stone didn't want anyone knowing how far he'd stepped over the line yet. He knew he'd have to come clean to his boss at some point but he'd cross that bridge when he came to it.

"Again I call bullshit. Have you fucked her?"

"What? No." Stone attempted to clear all emotion from his voice but he wanted to reach through the phone and wrap his hands around Jack's throat for talking the way he was. He didn't want anyone speaking about Soph and fucking. Unless it was him. *Shit.* "She's a job, Jack. Nothing more."

Stone turned around as Jack disguised the word "bullshit" as a cough in his ear—and found himself staring at a wide-eyed Soph.

Hurt swam in her gaze.

Fuck me.

"I gotta go." He hung up without bothering to wait for Jack's reply. "Hey."

She smiled but the curve of her lips resembled more of a twist. "Hey."

He kept his gaze on her as she moved past him to her suitcase and pulled out a shirt and pants.

He didn't protest when she slipped into the clothes. Didn't argue when she walked to the far side of the bed and crawled beneath the covers. Couldn't offer a word when she curled up on her side, facing away from him.

The urge to punch the wall had him fisting his hands at his sides. He'd screwed up. First by touching her and now by saying what they'd done was nothing.

He needed to tell her she was more important than a quick fuck but his tumbling mind couldn't come up with the words.

With a sigh, he scrubbed a hand over the back of his head and wondered if he should crawl in beside her, or put his clothes on and take the chair as he had last night.

It took him a few minutes to decide which was the better option. He checked the lock on the door and moved the chair against it for an added barrier. Checked the window was shut and locked and made sure the curtains were properly drawn.

He thumbed through his phone, checked his messages and emails. Shot off his nightly check-in email to Chip.

Finally he was out of things to procrastinate with.

Glancing at the bed, Stone contemplated the likelihood of Soph kicking him out of it and decided it—*she*—was worth the risk.

CHAPTER 10

Sophie held her breath as Stone slipped in to the bed behind her.

She wasn't sure why his words cut so deeply. She couldn't—shouldn't—expect anything, despite the amazing sex they'd had or the connection she'd felt when he was deep inside her.

They'd known each other twenty-four hours, and while he returned her attraction, he didn't return her affections.

And really, who fell for a guy in one day?

Rolling her lips between her teeth to keep her sigh inside, she admitted *she* did.

God. She was a cliché.

She'd fallen for her bodyguard.

Reginald would yell at her for sure. And she didn't even want to think about what her parents would say. Not that they'd say much beyond asking when their next check was coming. She couldn't stop the sigh this time.

"Come here."

The bed dipped and Stone's arm slid under her and curled around her waist, his hand splaying over her belly, while his other hand smoothed over her hip. With the gentlest of tugs, he pulled her back against him.

"Relax. You're safe."

She wasn't worried about that. Sophie knew, without a doubt, he'd keep her physically safe. It was emotionally she was concerned about.

She'd have thought by now she'd have a thicker hide, be less likely to let anyone get too deep and hurt her.

She'd been in the music industry for years, had seen the way some celebrities were chewed up and spat out, had witnessed numerous meltdowns and humiliations, and not once had she thought she'd be a victim.

From the very beginning, she'd shielded herself.

Hard not to erect emotional walls when her parents were money-grabbing, fame-seeking, coattail-riding para-sites. It was one of the only things she could thank them for.

They'd toughened her up with their so called 'affection' and really, most days the world had nothing on the two people who'd donated their DNA to make her.

Stone squeezed her closer and nuzzles behind her ear. "You're more."

Shutting her eyes tight, she held still.

"I've broken every rule with you. I should take myself off the job—"

"No!" She tried to turn and face him.

He slipped his arms more securely around her and held

her in place. "I'm not going anywhere. If Ford tried to make me, I'd quit and stay with you regardless of what he said."

"Why?" He was saying all the right words to soothe her wounded feelings but it wasn't enough. She'd never felt so exposed—so raw—so dependent on someone else's motives. "Why would you quit your job for someone you just met?"

He laughed softly, his breath ruffling her hair and making her shiver. "I'm asking myself the same question. All I know is I can't walk away from you."

"So now what?"

"Now. We get some sleep and tomorrow we go spend the day at the festival."

"We're going out again?" She tried not to get her hopes up, while the room Alice had given them wasn't bad it still felt like a jail cell to her. "I thought you wanted me to stay out of sight."

"I'll be right beside you and Jack is shadowing us. Plus, I don't think Hagar will do anything to draw attention to himself, and grabbing you at a crowded festival would definitely get him noticed."

"Does anyone know where he is?" The uncertainty, the not knowing when or if he'd find her... She shivered.

"No one has seen him since you did in LA."

"Do you think he's given up?" Sophie held her breath. She knew what answer she wanted, but she wasn't stupid and expected a different one.

"No."

"Bloody hell." She blew out her breath. "I knew you'd say that but I wish you hadn't."

"I promised I wouldn't lie to you."

"I know. I might wish you hadn't but I'd rather not like the answer than have you lie to me."

"If that's the case I'll tell you now that I plan to call Jack in the morning to work out the best way to get you noticed while keeping you safe. We need to flush Hagar out of hiding. It's the fastest way to put an end to this."

"So I'm bait?"

"No. You're the prize. He wants you. We'll make him believe he can have you."

Revulsion slithered through her, making her shudder.

"He can't have you." Stone's hold tightened. "You're mine."

A shiver—the good kind—raced through her when Stone uttered the last two words in a guttural growl.

The possession in his tone, his words, gave her a sensual buzz and she remembered how he'd taken her earlier. As though he couldn't get enough of her. As if he wanted to pound some sort of claim into her.

When he said things—did things—like that, she couldn't be blamed for falling. In spite of knowing so little about each other, she felt a connection deeper than she had with anyone else in the past or present.

"Go to sleep, Soph."

"I don't think I can."

"Try. I promise you're safe."

"I know. That's not what's keeping me awake."

"Do you want to talk about it?"

She smiled. "No. Can we talk about something else?"

"Sure. What do you want to talk about?"

"Anything."

"Okay."

They were quiet for a bit. The night noises outside the window the only sound breaking the silence around them. Finally she decided on a question.

"What's with your name? Did you change it?"

"Stone Mason is my birth name."

"It's a little unusual."

"More than a little." He chuckled and rubbed his hand lazily over her stomach. "My mother was—*is*—a little more than a hippy. She's the poster woman for out-there."

"And your dad didn't argue?"

"I doubt she cared what he thought. Not that she knew who my dad was. She could narrow it down to five choices."

"What?" This time she wiggled and squirmed until he loosened his hold and she managed to turn in his arms and face him. "That's...it's...I..."

Stone laughed. "Yeah. She was all about the free love. Still is."

Sophie had no idea what to say. Her parents might not be the best but at least she knew who they were.

"Don't worry. Not knowing who my dad was didn't make a difference to me. Still doesn't. The commune where I grew up had plenty of male role models, and as I said, free love was a big part of the community's values, so I never lacked for a father figure."

"You grew up in a commune?" The thought boggled her mind. "Do you have brothers or sisters?"

"Not from my mother. I'm the only one. My biological father could have more kids though. Some of the kids I grew up with could have been my half siblings but it wouldn't have mattered. We were treated the same by everyone. All the adults raised us as though we were theirs."

"So you had lots of mums and dads and brothers and sisters?"

"Pretty much. It was a good way to grow up. We were cherished by all, and other than having very limited contact with the outside world, the commune wasn't a bad place to live."

"I'm gobsmacked. Just the idea seems unreal to me."

"It is to most people."

"Where was the commune?"

"On a huge property on the north coast of New South Wales. Inland a bit from Byron Bay."

"Does your mother still live there?"

"Yes. She's still in the timber shack I was born in."

"Timber shack?"

"Better than the tent she was in *before* I came along."

"Did you at least have running water? Hot water? Plumbed sewage?" Sophie had been camping once, when she was a teenager, with the family of a school friend, and the lack of plumbing had been enough to turn her off the outdoor adventure for life. "I'm not really a nature person. I don't think I could live away from civilization like that."

"We weren't *that* cut off from the world. There was a

washhouse next to the kitchen house. We had electricity too. Definitely not primitive. And the closest town was only a twenty minute drive away. If we couldn't find what we needed there the city was an hour farther."

"Would you take me there?" As soon as the words left her mouth, she wanted to suck them back in.

"Sure. We can go there as soon as Hagar is out of the picture. I've got holidays owed."

"You'd really take me?"

"If you want to go."

Sophie tipped her head back and brushed her lips on Stone's chin. "Thank you."

"For?"

"Being honest. Sharing."

She felt, more than saw him shrug. "No big deal."

"It is. You said yourself you've broken rules."

"I'd break more." Stone slid a hand up her spine to the back of her head. Applying pressure, he moved her until her face was tucked into his neck. "I don't know what we're doing or where we're going, but I can't walk away from you even when I know I'm losing my objectivity."

Sophie wanted to tell him everything would be okay. Wanted it to *be* okay. Except she didn't completely understand his job or the potential threat of the man stalking her. She had to put herself in Stone's care and hope that whatever this was brewing between them, it didn't diminish his skills.

And put her life—or his—at risk.

CHAPTER 11

STONE SPOTTED Jack two booths behind them, mindful of not acknowledging the other man, he skimmed his gaze straight past.

Their plan relied on Hagar not discovering their relationship—or anyone else, for that matter. As far as anyone knew, Stone and Soph were a normal couple out enjoying the gorgeous summer day.

They'd arrived at the festival about thirty minutes ago. Wandering from booth to booth, they'd admired crafts, eaten local food, and even partaken in a local beverage known as Melt. The last had been an under-the-table transaction that had him raising his eyebrows but sampling anyway.

He'd barely had a sip but the alcohol content was so potent, he'd taken a punch to the gut as though he'd slung back a keg of the stuff. He could imagine the locals—and presumably a good number of out-of-towners—getting well and truly hammered on the town's brand of moonshine.

Not that anyone needed to get drunk for Winter Lake's annual Ice Breaker Festival to be a hit. Lake Front Park and the barricaded road were wall-to-wall people.

Locals and visitors laughed and ate, drank and had a great time. Kids ran here and there, parents trailing behind. It was a kaleidoscope of faces and so far neither he, nor Soph, nor Jack had seen the one visitor they sought.

Hagar.

Not that any of them had a clear idea of what the man looked like.

Chip had managed to get a copy of the image taken by Customs when Hagar exited Australia, but once again his features were indistinguishable due to the full beard he'd worn.

How Landlocked's resident computer geek got into a government system to obtain the picture Stone didn't know, and was safer *not* knowing. Although he had to admit having a computer genius at their disposal worked in their favor, regardless of his possibly illegal methods.

After studying the image Chip had acquired, the entire Landlocked team came to the same conclusion. Hagar's beard was fake.

Unfortunately, the computer-altered image of Hagar minus facial hair wasn't a good one. A five-year-old could do better with a crayon and paper.

Okay, not really, but the frustration of not knowing exactly who they were looking for was getting to Stone.

He liked to know his enemy. Looks, behavior, location.

Currently he knew none of those things about Soph's stalker, and to say he was edgy was an understatement.

"Here. Try this." Soph shoved a stick of corn in front of his face.

His stomach cramped in protest. She'd been buying every food item on offer since they'd gotten here. He took the latest offering with a forced smile. "Thanks."

"Don't thank me until you eat it."

Stone arched an eyebrow as he brought the sweet-smelling corn to his mouth.

"It might taste like crap." She smirked at him.

Ready to take a bite, he said, "I find that hard to believe. It's corn on the cob. You just boil it, right? How can you screw that up?"

She shrugged a bare shoulder. "How would I know? Do I look like a chef to you?"

He sank his teeth into hot, juicy corn and glanced down her body. Starting with her smooth shoulders, exposed by her sleeveless dress, he moved down her chest to the lush curves of her breasts, where they peaked out of her low-cut neckline, and felt himself harden at the thought of having those beauties in his mouth again.

In fear of developing a hard-on he couldn't hide in public, he reversed his gaze and met her stare head-on. "No. Chef is not what I think when I look at you."

She laughed. A rich, deep, joy-soaked sound that rang around them, drawing gazes and making Stone want to hear it all the time.

Smiling, he placed a hand on her lower back and urged her forward. "C'mon, let's walk over to the local animal display and petting zoo. See if we can't find your inner nature lover."

Soph's nose scrunched up. "It'll smell over there, and I'd better not get anything other than a little dirt on these shoes."

He looked at her shoes. Definitely not footwear for mountain country but she'd insisted on wearing them and the sexy dress when they'd gotten ready earlier. "I'm more worried about you breaking an ankle than getting them dirty."

"Said like a typical man."

"In case you missed the memo, I am a man."

She shot him a sultry smile. "Oh, don't worry. I got that memo. I got it *gooood*," she sang with a flutter of her lashes.

Stone laughed, slipped his arm around her shoulders, and pulled her into his side. "I'll resend it after we deal with Hagar."

Pouting up at him, Soph grumbled, "I was hoping you'd resend it when we got back to the room."

He couldn't think of anything better except he'd decided not to cross that line again. Not until she was safe and the threat to her no longer in play.

He'd even made the decision not to purchase any more condoms. They'd used his one and only last night so they'd have to abstain until he could cover that threat too.

"I'm going to assume your silence means we won't be re-examining your man card this evening."

The excited chatter of children gave him the perfect opportunity to ignore her remark. He steered Soph around a group of adults and off to the side where they could see what was going on. Peering into the penned area, Stone saw a bunch of fluff balls racing around on the grass.

"Kittens!" Soph squealed beside him. "Oh my god, they're so cute. I want one."

"Um... Not a nature lover, remember?" He moved her in front of him so she could see better.

"Don't need to be to have a kitten."

"I guess not but I believe Customs and Quarantine might have a problem with you taking one of those home."

"Bloody hell. I didn't even think about that." She leaned over the small fence and dangled her hand in, trying to pat one of the blurs of fur as it zipped past. "Wow, they're fast."

He couldn't believe he was going to say it, but... "You could get one when you get back to Australia."

"Oh. I could." She looked over her shoulder at him, her bright smile flashing for a second before it faded. "But I'm not home a lot of the time. It's why I don't already have a cat, or a dog. I've never had a pet, actually. Not even a goldfish."

Stone wanted to kiss that frown right off her face and get her any damn pet she wanted. Wanted to tell her he'd take care of them when she wasn't home, but then he realized if he was home and she wasn't, they wouldn't be together, and that wasn't what *he* wanted.

He hated the idea of not being able to make her happy.

His whole thought process struck him as bizarre. He wanted to be her savior, and not just because it was his job.

Things between him and Soph were complicated and

tangled beyond his understanding. Figuring it all out would have to wait.

Before anything else, they had to remove the threat Hagar represented. Then he had to make sure she was safe from any other nutjob who fixated on her.

Stone cupped her elbow. "C'mon. Finish up your corn so we can take a ride on the Ferris wheel."

"You heard what Alice said happens up there, right?"

He grinned at her and moved his hand to hers, lacing their fingers. "Sure did." He couldn't wait to get her up there and steal a kiss. Maybe a little more.

"I might not want to ride the wheel with *you*," she said as he pulled her along beside him.

"Yes, you do." Stone was confident of that. Besides, if she didn't want to ride with him now, he knew how to convince her she didn't want to get off by the time they reached the top.

"Cocky."

"Not yet but I will be when we *get off*." He emphasized the last two words and added an eyebrow waggle for good measure.

Soph's laughter floated behind them as they meandered through the crowd.

They reached the ticket booth and Stone got in line while Soph disposed of their finished corncobs in a trashcan two feet away. It was the most distance he'd allow between them.

When it was his turn, he handed over a few bills and received a bunch of tickets in return. Pulling Soph away from the booth, he waved the tickets in her face and said, "Ready to take a ride?"

"I'm ready to ride you anytime, anywhere," she whispered while gazing at him through lowered lashes.

He sucked in a breath as fire licked at his balls. "Fuck, woman, you keep that up and you'll be getting more than a kiss up there."

"Promises, promises." She sashayed off toward the entry gate, her ass swaying nicely under the flirty skirt of her dress, her legs looking killer in those sky-high shoes.

Damn. He was in trouble.

It didn't matter what he'd decided. He was stopping at the store and buying a box of condoms.

There was no way they were staying in the same room tonight without him getting her naked and under him again.

CHAPTER 12

SOPHIE SLID across the smooth plastic seat to the far side of the carriage and laughed at the look on Stone's face.

"You think being all the way over there is going to stop me?" he asked, a twinkle of mischief in his eyes.

"Can't make it too easy for you." She tipped her head down to hide a smile and peered at him through her lashes. The seat rocked and rose a few feet before stopping.

Curling his hand around her thigh, he tugged her toward him as he moved closer and whispered, "Nothing easy about you."

When it came to Stone, she was pretty sure the *best* description for her was easy-peasy. For heaven's sake, she'd had sex with the man within two days of laying eyes on him.

Not that she regretted it—nothing to regret about the passion she'd experienced under his focused attention—but it didn't get much easier than that.

"Don't say it." Two fingers covered her mouth. "Sleeping with me so soon after we met doesn't make you *easy*."

That he was in sync with her thoughts brought her up short. She knew it was his job to read situations—people—but he seemed to read her with far too little difficulty. "I'm not sure I like you being in my head."

"You have an expressive face." He trailed a fingertip along her temple. "And your eyes are like windows to every thought that flashes through that pretty head of yours."

"See..." A shiver tiptoed down her spine. "Easy," she murmured as that teasing finger drifted down her cheek then trailed across her lips.

"I don't like the way your lips are turned down. We should fix that." He leaned in and Sophie pulled back to keep their mouths from connecting.

"I could be frowning because I'm scared of heights and you've dragged me on this thing."

She waved her hand around them then crossed her arms and distanced herself farther. She wasn't afraid of heights exactly but she was definitely grateful this Ferris wheel was one with enclosed seating, not those stupid hang-in-the-air chairs.

"Or maybe I have indigestion."

Stone laughed, the deep male rumble sending a flutter through her belly. "Indigestion is definitely in the cards with the food we've eaten in the last hour. And I won't mention how much *you* packed away..."

He glanced down her torso, skimming his gaze to her

toes and back again, his eyes alight with lust when they locked on hers once more.

"I don't know where you put it all. There isn't a spare ounce on you."

Another shiver stole through her. It had nothing to do with the cold breeze blowing in from over the frozen lake.

On the contrary. Right now, Sophie was experiencing what she'd heard older women refer to as a hot flash, except her personal heat wave wasn't brought on by menopause. Men no pause necessary here.

Or in this case, man no pause needed.

Shaking her head at the ease with which he aroused her, she laughed. "I'm sorry. You're wrong. I'm *so* easy when it comes to you."

He leaned closer. "How easy?" he murmured against her cheek.

"Put your hand up my skirt and find out."

She couldn't believe how daring she was with Stone. He made her think and feel and want on a level no one else had.

His gaze fastened on hers as their carriage jerked and started to rise again. Her breathing grew shallower with every inch the ground dropped away beneath them, but it was the look in Stone's eyes that had her heart racing, her nipples puckering, and her sex clenching.

"Stone."

"A couple more seconds..."

Halfway to the top, he dove in. His mouth slanted over hers and his hand swept up the inside of her thigh, his fingertips finding the damp strip of cloth between her legs and stroking in a frustratingly light caress.

Shifting in her seat, she moved against his touch in an attempt to increase the pressure—to take the pleasure deeper.

He pulled his hand away and spoke against her mouth. "Not so fast."

"Stone." Sophie didn't care that she was begging. She'd get on her knees if it would make him press a little harder. A little faster.

"I like it when you beg in that sexy silk voice. Especially when my fingers are wet and buried between your legs." He nipped her bottom lip.

She gasped with the sharp jolt of pleasure-pain. "They're not buried anywhere."

He laughed and slipped two fingers beneath the side of her undies near her hip. Sliding them slowly down and over the throbbing flesh of her sex, he asked, "Better?"

"More." She rocked her hips. "Inside."

His lips trailed along her jawline toward her ear. "You want more? Here?"

"Yes..." she hissed as he drove a finger into her clenching channel.

"How close are you?" Stone licked her ear, added a second finger. "Can you get off in the next few seconds?"

Sophie couldn't comprehend his words. Every functioning brain cell was awash with sensation, with an urgent need her body was desperate to sate. "Please."

Stone's fingers plunged in and out and his thumb found

her clit, circled, pressed, and flicked. "C'mon, Soph, I know it's there."

He strummed and stroked and pushed and took her to the edge with astonishing speed.

Her body tightened, clamped down, and froze for a split second before it seemed to burst wide open and shatter into a million trillion pieces. She buried her face in Stone's neck, her cry of passion muffled against his skin.

"God, you're fucking perfect." His fingers slowed, the friction and pressure less and less with each slide of his skin on hers. "Snuggle in close. We're near the ground again."

Near the ground? *Bloody hell.* They were still on the Ferris wheel. The man had skills. And she was way easier than easy-peasy.

Shuddering with aftershocks, Sophie kept her face tucked into his neck and wrapped her arms around his waist.

"We're going up again," Stone murmured into her hair, his lips pressing down quickly before he shifted her in his arms and sat her across his lap.

There was no missing the erection bulging beneath his jeans; it pressed into the side of her thigh in a hot brand of temptation that her recent orgasm did nothing to weaken. "Stone?"

"I'm good."

Rolling her head on his shoulder, Sophie searched his gaze. "But—"

"I'm good." He smiled. "Better than good. Just need you to ride a little longer with me."

"I can do that."

She wanted to argue but the noise of the festival had finally infiltrated the passion fog in her head and Sophie smiled even as her cheeks heated with a combination of embarrassment and arousal when she remembered where they were. What she'd let him do to her.

In public.

She hoped the solid bottom half of the enclosure hid them from view.

"We're going to stop soon. We were the second-to-last ones on so it'll be a few stops before we get to the ground."

As he said the words, the carriage jerked beneath them, rocking to a standstill a few meters off the ground, as the riders two seats below them were let off.

Turning her head, Sophie's gaze moved over the people milling around in front of the Ferris wheel—and locked on the creepy blue gaze of her worst nightmare.

Recoiling, she sucked in a breath and choked on a scream as she scrambled away from the man who'd taken away her sense of safety and replaced it with fear.

"Soph?" Stone grabbed her shoulders and kept her from climbing off his lap. "Soph, what's wrong?"

"Him." Air wheezed through her constricted throat, tangled in her vocal cords. "Him. I-it's *him.*"

Stone's head spun around and he moved his torso to hide her behind him. "Where?"

"Right there. In front of us." The seat jerked and they began the upward climb again.

"I don't see him." He leaned to the side and peered through the bars, his gaze scanning the crowd walking around beneath the Ferris wheel. Sitting back, he dug his phone from his pocket and quickly made a call.

"Soph just spotted Hagar at the base of the Ferris wheel. To the north. I didn't set eyes on him though."

Sophie couldn't hear what Jack said and Stone's side of the conversation buzzed in her ears like the drone of a thousand bees.

He *was* here.

He'd found her just as Stone had said.

CHAPTER 13

STONE USHERED Soph into their room and shut and locked the door behind them. She hadn't spoken a word since they were on the Ferris wheel and he was beginning to worry. He pulled her into his arms and drew her as close as he could—held her tight.

"It's okay. I won't let him near you," he promised for the hundredth time since he'd coaxed her off the ride.

She trembled in his arms and Stone had the urge to smash something.

Preferably Hagar's face.

He hated that the man could frighten her into muteness. In the last few days he'd discovered an animated, happy woman who enjoyed life to the fullest and didn't deserve to have her world disrupted by a deranged man.

His phone rang and as much as he didn't want to let her go, he knew he had to. "That'll be Jack. I need to answer it," he murmured into her hair.

Soph nodded and pulled out of his embrace. Her head was lowered so he couldn't see her eyes, couldn't read what she was thinking. Wanting to keep her close, he felt disappointment shoot through him when she walked to the far side of the bed and lay down. She curled into a ball and tucked her hands beneath her chin.

She looked so small, so vulnerable—so broken.

The desire to punch Hagar's face morphed into a dangerous need to render harm to every inch of the man. Slowly. Over and over again.

Yanking his phone from his pocket, he hit accept and put the device to his ear. "Tell me you found the fucker," he growled in greeting.

"Not a sign of him. Is she sure it was him?"

"You saw her, man, there's no way a *possible* sighting could instill that much fear."

"Yeah. I know. It's just..." Jack's frustration echoed Stone's. "I didn't like this prick before. I *really* don't like him now."

"Get in line."

"He's taunting her."

"I know. I'm just not sure why. He's been following her for longer than the last week; you saw those walls of photos —this isn't a new thing. I can't work out what his game is though."

"I've been running through everything I know about stalkers over and over and not managed to peg this guy. The meal he left her threw me too. But...I think I've worked it out. I don't think he's out to hurt her or scare her."

"Well, he's fucking that up," Stone growled, his eyes glued to the woman curled in on herself on the bed.

"He is, but I don't think he knows that. Not yet anyway." Jack sucked in a breath. "How is she?"

"Hard to say. Not a word yet."

"We need her to tell us what he looked like. What he was wearing. Anything."

"I don't want to push her right now. Give me some time. Let her process it and realize she's safe. It had to be a shock to see him watching her. I have no doubt he placed himself right in her line of sight. Wanted her to know he was there. God knows how long he was watching us."

"Fuck, I hate this prick. Try and get whatever you can out of her but I'll be honest, I don't think it'll help now anyway. He's crawled back under whatever rock he's been hiding under." Jack sighed. "For now he can't get at her even if he knows where she is. I'll do another sweep of downtown then head your way and scout around. Are you sure he's not staying at the Lodge?"

"As positive as I can be with this guy. And no one followed us here. I made sure of that."

"I don't like it. There're too many variables with all those people renting rooms. Not to mention the employees."

"None of the guests match Hagar, plus they were all here before Soph came to town, and the employees checked out when Chip did his thing."

"Still not happy about your location but for now it'll have to do. I'll let you know when I'm on-site."

"I'm locking down for the night."

"I've got your back."

"Thanks."

Disconnecting, Stone dropped his phone on the foot of the bed as he made his way around to Soph's side. Crouching down, he brushed her hair back at her temple.

"Hey. How you doing?"

"Okay."

Her croaky reply took him by surprise, but filled him with relief. "Found your voice, I see."

She flashed him a wobbly smile.

"What do you need?"

"A gun."

Stone grinned. "We talked about this. You're not getting your hands on my gun."

"Bloody hell." There was no strength in her words, none of her usual spirit. It was as though her normal vitality had been sucked right out of her.

"C'mon. Let's get you in a bath." Hopefully the heat would relax her, make it easier for her to find her spark again.

Stone didn't like seeing her defeated. He wanted her to fight back now that she wasn't quivering in fear.

She let him help her sit up. "Will you wash my back?" she asked.

His gaze met hers, her twinkly eyes lifting a load of tension from his body. Smiling, he said, "If you want me to."

"I want your hands on me. I want to feel something other than numb. I *need* it. I don't want him to take more than he already has."

"Okay." He helped her to her feet. "But no sex."

She eyed him with a narrowed gaze—a deep frown.

"It's not that I don't want you." The hard-on in his pants was proof he did.

Her eyelids fluttered closed and she drew in a deep breath. Eyes popping open again, she stared at him with those brutally honest green orbs that took his legs out from under him. She was so open. No shields. No hiding.

"It's okay. I get it. You think you'd be taking advantage of me."

"No. That's not it."

"It's not?"

"I can't protect you." He shrugged. "I only had one condom with me."

"Oh." She took a step, pressed her front to his and sent a shudder of desire rushing though him. "We can do other things besides actual intercourse though, right?"

Stone sucked in a breath when she wiggled so her breasts rubbed against his chest. "You're dangerous when you want something, you know that?"

She grinned with some of the sparkle he'd grown to love. "It's you. You bring out the best in me," she drawled in a sexy whisper before shooting him a wink.

He chuckled. "I'm sure others would say it's the worst. You have an image that doesn't include having sex with your bodyguard."

"I've never worried about what other people think."

Tilting his head to the side, he asked, "So you don't care what I think?"

"You aren't other people."

"I'm not?"

"No."

"Then what am I?"

"The guy I'm falling for."

God. She slayed him.

Her honesty. Her refusal to hide an ounce of herself from him. Every fucking thing about her brought him to his knees and he had no defense against the emotions she inspired.

He didn't want any.

But he wasn't stupid. He knew the situation could be responsible for their chemistry.

Stone understood himself well and knew what he felt was real—solid—but Soph, for all her honesty, remained an unknown, and while he believed she felt something for him, he wasn't convinced it would last beyond their forced time together.

And right there was another reason he shouldn't touch her again. With or without protection, intercourse or no intercourse, he should keep his hands to himself and do his job—only his job. For now.

"Soph—"

"Don't say it." She put her hand over his mouth. "I don't want to hear anything that isn't going to give me what I want—what I *need*—and right now I want to have that bath you offered. With you."

Stone closed his eyes and tried to do the right thing but she did that wiggly move again, whispered "Please, Stone," in that silky seductress voice of hers and any restraint he might have held on to dissolved like ice on a hot tin roof. He heard his control snap like the crack of lightning.

Opening his eyes, he grabbed her hand. "C'mon."

"Yes!"

He snorted. "And you think *you're* the easy one," he muttered.

She had him wrapped around her little finger. He was man enough to accept that...not reckless enough to admit it out loud.

CHAPTER 14

Sophie leaned back and swirled her hands in the warm water, skimming her fingertips over Stone's thighs.

His arms rested lazily around her waist, his fingers laced together just below her belly button, and his chest supported her spine, his legs bracketing hers.

He surrounded her completely. Made her feel safe.

They'd been relaxing in the big old tub for about twenty minutes and she was done thinking—overthinking.

Her thoughts were only going in circles now anyway.

"I'm tired of waiting for him to do something." The quiet words echoed off the tile walls as though she'd shouted.

Stone stirred against her, his chest rising with a deep indrawn breath.

"I want to go back to the festival tomorrow. See if we can flush him out in the open again. Maybe you could leave me alone for a few minutes—"

"*No.*"

There was no point arguing. Stone's word lived up to his name. Rock hard without a soft spot to be found. There would be no changing his mind on that point but she had to convince him they needed—*she* needed—to face this guy.

If she showed Hagar she wasn't frightened, that he didn't scare her, he might leave her alone.

"I'm not staying locked away any longer. I can't."

"I'm not leaving you alone."

"Okay."

"That was too easy." He gripped her waist and pushed her up. Lifting her out of the water completely, he said, "Turn around. I want to see your face while we have this conversation."

Bloody hell.

He'd proven he could read her every thought already. She didn't stand a chance of keeping anything from him if he was looking her in the eye.

Not that she wanted to hide anything from Stone. She just didn't want him to see her fear. She might be ready to face this guy head-on but that didn't mean she wasn't scared of what might happen.

Resigned to the inevitable, she sighed and spun around. She lowered back into the water until her knees rested on the bottom of the tub on either side of his hips.

"Now tell me exactly what you're thinking," he demanded.

"I don't want to live in fear anymore. I've always gone after what I want, and I want my life back. I'm tired of looking over my shoulder, of waiting for the other shoe to drop. I gave this Hagar person control by allowing him to get to me, by letting him dictate my actions."

"He's dangerous."

"We don't know that."

"I know his type."

"Maybe. But you can't be sure, and I'm done hiding out. He seems to find me regardless of where I go. I want this over with. Now."

She watched him fight an internal battle that tightened his jaw and put worry wrinkles in his forehead.

Sophie couldn't tell if he was going to agree with her or not and she honestly couldn't say which outcome she really wanted to hear.

He sat up, one hand gripping her hip, the other sliding up her back to cradle her neck. "Okay. But we need a plan. I'll call Jack—"

"Not now. Tomorrow."

"I thought you wanted this over?"

"I do but it makes sense to do whatever it is we're going to do in daylight and we're running out of that today." She could see the sky darkening through the small high window above the bath.

Stone sighed. "You're right. We'll call Jack first thing tomorrow. Make a plan before breakfast." He pulled her down against him using the hand at her neck, the arm at her hip wrapping around her and pressing them together tighter. He kissed the top of her head and held her close.

They lay there, skin on skin, each in their own

thoughts, until the water cooled to an uncomfortable temperature and Sophie started to shiver.

"Time to get out." Stone rose to his feet, Sophie cradled in his arms as though she were an extension of his body and not an extra burden to lift.

She wrapped her legs around his waist, her arms around his neck and held on as he stepped over the side of the tub. "Are we going to bed now?" she asked hopefully.

He looked down at her for a moment then shook his head. "We said no sex."

"*You* said no sex, I said we could do other things. Besides, I'm pretty sure your cock has other ideas."

"Ignore it. I am."

Sophie laughed. Hard to ignore the thick shaft trapped between their bodies.

He'd been hard from the minute they'd taken their clothes off, and while he'd done an admirable job of ignoring it—as had she—it was one more thing she was tired of.

Putting her desire for Stone aside hadn't been working anyway; no point continuing the futile effort.

Now that she'd come to a decision about her stalker she wanted to fix other things in her life.

Namely the pulse of desire that always thrummed in her veins when Stone was around.

"I'm on the pill."

Stone's stride stuttered, his hands clenching on her ass where he held her tight against him. "What?" he croaked.

"You heard me."

His eyes closed on a long exhalation. "Soph."

"I want you. Nothing between us. Just tonight. I don't need or want more than that."

"You should want more." His eyes opened, his fiery gaze locking with hers. "You *deserve* more."

"Yes. I do, and I should, but I'll take tonight. Tomorrow isn't here yet. I'll worry about it when it is."

She didn't want to beg him to sleep with her. There were other ways she could persuade him. Except she hoped he wanted her as badly as she wanted him and wouldn't need convincing.

Eyelids dropping to half-mast, Stone stared at her with molten eyes. "I can't seem to say no to you."

"Then don't."

He remained quiet, studying her for so long she couldn't curb the urge to fill the silence.

"Don't be my bodyguard. Don't be the guy hired to protect me. Be Stone Mason, the man. What does he want? What would he do right now?"

"He would have you in bed already."

"Then take me there. Just you and me. Stone and Sophie. Not the bodyguard, not the pop star. Forget everything and everyone outside of this room, outside of us."

"God. You take me to my knees."

"I'd rather be on mine." Images of being at his feet flashed through her mind. Memories flooded her with heat and want and the need to taste him again.

"Fuck, woman."

"Yes. Fuck your woman."

His eyes flashed, his nostrils flared, and a groan rumbled in his throat before he took her mouth with his.

He sucked the breath right out of her. Shot her from simmering arousal to boiling need with a few strokes of his tongue.

Tearing his mouth from hers, he panted, "Bed. Now."

Sophie laughed. "You're the one with your feet on the floor."

With a growl, Stone charged toward the bed where he took them down, caging her beneath him. "Not on the floor now."

"We're getting the bed wet."

"Don't care."

Before she could say another word his mouth slanted over hers. He didn't go slow, didn't allow for protest. No, Stone's kiss took, demanded surrender, and Sophie gave. Willingly.

She'd hold nothing back from this man. Whatever he wanted he could take. Whatever he needed she would give.

And whatever happened tomorrow she would accept.

Because tonight was theirs. Every hour, every minute, every second. They would forget about the world outside these walls, forget about everything except each other.

CHAPTER 15

STONE COULDN'T BREATHE. Couldn't think. But damn he could feel.

Every inch of her against him, under him, inside him.

Sophie Collins had dug in deep. She'd wiggled her way beneath his skin, burrowed into his bones, and left her name in permanent ink across his heart—his soul.

He didn't know what would happen tomorrow. Didn't care when he had her naked and willing on the bed with him now.

She'd given him more than her body. He might not be certain about her heart, but he had her trust.

She trusted him not just to keep her safe from a deranged stalker.

She trusted him enough to offer herself without anything between them.

He'd never been with a woman without protection. His mother might have been all about the free love and loving whoever you wanted to emotionally or physically but she'd all but beaten into him the need for safe sex.

Smiling against Soph's lips he murmured, "I'm clean." She needed to know he wouldn't take her trust lightly. "I have a yearly physical and I've never had sex without a condom."

Her hands cradled his face, held him still as she pulled back to look him in the eye. "Let's not talk about you having sex with other women."

"I want you to know—"

"Stone, do you think I'd offer to go without a condom if I thought you wouldn't be safe? I trust you on every level. I can't explain what it is, whether it's something you've done or do, I just know bone deep that you'll take care of me in any situation. *Every* situation."

He opened his mouth but Soph pressed both thumbs over his lips.

"No. Don't say I shouldn't or anything about us not knowing each other long. I've spent years working in an industry where everyone is after something; most of those that get close want a piece of you or to knock you out of the spotlight. It didn't take me long to recognize the genuine from the not." She smiled. "I. Trust. You."

Stone still couldn't breathe. His throat had closed up and his heart thumped so hard his chest ached. "Soph." Her name was a breath and if he hadn't already known he was falling for this woman, he did now. She'd given him something no one else ever had.

Herself.

Unconditionally.

"Make love to me, Stone."

His pounding heart stopped. Slammed into his ribs and ricocheted back like a pinball hitting the highest target in the machine.

She might not have said she loved him directly but he wasn't oblivious to the phrase she used or the look in her eyes.

He didn't want to get his hopes up that this was more than the circumstances they found themselves in except his heart and brain weren't listening to reason. As far as they—and his body—were concerned, Soph was his.

One hundred percent his.

And if everything came to a head tomorrow, if they found Hagar and removed the threat, he could lose her.

She wouldn't need him to keep her safe anymore.

He had tonight to mark her as deeply as she'd marked him.

He couldn't—wouldn't—let a second pass without making sure she knew how he felt.

He might not be ready to say the words out loud, and he doubted she'd believe them if he did, but he could show her with his body and his actions how important she was.

He'd make tonight about her. About cherishing her. Loving her. And when he finally allowed himself to sink inside her with nothing between them neither of them would be able to walk away.

CHAPTER 16

STONE COULDN'T SHAKE the dark cloud of foreboding that hung over him. Gut clenched and every muscle drawn tight, he scanned the crowd.

He'd let Jack and Soph talk him into this, into bringing her out for another day of festival fun, and with each tick of the clock, he regretted it more. He knew most of his anxiety stemmed from the fact Soph was no longer just a client.

He'd fallen in love with her.

It didn't matter that it was only days since they'd met. They'd connected. Deeply.

Last night had cemented that connection. She'd let him inside her with no barriers. He was too old and cynical to be awestruck by that alone, even if it was a first for him.

And her.

They'd taken that step together and in spite of common sense telling him whatever relationship they were forging couldn't be real under the circumstances, it was the most real he'd ever been with a woman.

"See anything?" Jack's voice rumbled in Stone's earpiece.

"Nothing yet."

"Sophie?"

"No signal yet." And he'd been watching for it. His eyes hadn't left her since she'd arrived with Alice and her daughter-in-law, Sadie. "She's talking with some local women Alice and Sadie introduced her to."

"How close are you?"

"Not close enough if something goes wrong," he barked.

"Suck it up, lover boy. She knows what to do if he gets hold of her."

"He better not *breathe* on her, never mind touch her."

Stone struggled to remain in place. The conversation alone had him on the brink of racing over to Soph, grabbing her, and getting out of here. His gut told him things were going to go south and he'd never ignored his instincts before.

Jack laughed. "You've got it bad."

So what if he did? It didn't change what they were here to do. Protect Soph. "Focus."

"Don't worry about me. I'm not seeing things through lust-fogged glasses."

"I can do my job."

"Never said you couldn't but if you don't dial back those emotions, you'll be distracted, and that's the last thing Sophie needs right now."

Stone knew Jack was right, knew he had to push his feelings aside and find his usual stone-like calm. "She's on the move."

"Got her."

He could trust Jack. Had done so on numerous occasions, but this time the stakes were higher and they both knew it.

"I've got eyes on her too."

Stone moved around a family with three small kids. Almost tripped over the littlest one as she darted away from her father.

"I'm to the north of you both. Closer to her than you."

Stone spotted Jack among the many faces. "I got you. Any sign of our target?"

"Nothing."

"Where the hell is he?" he growled.

"Give it some time. We haven't been here an hour yet."

It felt like days. "They're stopping again."

Stone paused at the stall of a local artist. Pretended to admire the sculptures covering the booth's table while he kept an eye on Soph.

She didn't seem nervous. In fact, she was laughing and talking as though she didn't have a care in the world.

"At least one of us is having fun," he muttered.

"That's made from locally sourced timber and scrap metal."

He glanced up to find an old guy smiling at him. His weathered face spoke of years in the sun, many hours smiling.

"They're good," Stone offered without much enthusiasm. He didn't want to start up a conversation. He had to stay on task.

"My grandson is the artist. Never really got into art myself, but the kid does all right with it."

Stone smiled and turned to see Soph, Alice, and Sadie moving again.

"I'll come back later."

He tried to be polite but a group of teenagers moved between him and Soph, and Stone's heart damn near beat right out of his chest when he lost sight of her.

Darting around the rowdy group, he picked up his pace and spoke into his mic, "I've lost visual."

"I've got her. They're heading for the house of ice."

"House of ice?"

"Affirmative."

Shit. "Jesus. How the hell do we keep eyes on her in there?"

"I'll go in right behind. You need to stay back. Hagar saw you with her yesterday so you're a known entity."

He didn't want to let Jack take the lead but it made sense if they wanted to give the illusion Soph was on her own—defenseless.

"Roger," he agreed reluctantly.

"There's a crowd. Not sure I like this…"

The uncertainty in Jack's voice ramped up Stone's anxiety another notch. "Should we abort?"

"No. I'm right on her." Jack's voice lowered. "No one between us."

"Don't hesitate to grab her and pull her out," Stone ordered.

"Guaranteed."

"You want me inside or near the exit?"

"Outside."

Jack didn't say 'just in case' but Stone heard it and his insides spiraled tighter.

He spotted Soph's high ponytail with its bright red ribbon and his nerves took a jolt before relief flowed through him. Just the sight of her made breathing easier.

"I see her." Jack moved behind her, blocking Stone's view. "And you."

"We're going in," Jack said in spite of the fact he knew Stone could see them now.

"Talk me through it." If he couldn't be inside with her, he'd use Jack as his eyes and ears.

"Shit."

Stone lurched forward. "What?"

"All good. A headless dummy dropped from the ceiling. Scared the shit out of all of us. I think this is some sort of haunted ice house. The women are together. Laughing."

Stone could hear screams, rattling chains, moaning wails, as well as a hiss he assumed was from a fake smoke machine through his earpiece. "You still with her?"

"Yeah. We're moving into the next section."

"Keep talking." Stone paced a six-foot span at the side of the tent that housed the ice house. "I need to hear what's happening."

"Someone has gone to a lot of effort to try to scare the pants off people but all your girl is doing is laughing her ass off."

Stone smiled.

"Shit."

"What?"

"Dammit. She's through to the next section but I'm caught behind a group of old ladies."

"Get in there!" Stone cursed under his breath, spun around to charge inside—

And came face-to-face with Ford Moreland.

What the fuck was his boss doing here?

"Stone." Ford tipped his chin.

He cleared his throat. "Ford."

"Where's our client?"

"Inside. Jack's on her."

"I hear you are too."

Crap. Stone didn't know how to reply to that. He'd thought about what he'd say to Ford when he and Soph returned to Australia, but he hadn't nailed down the words yet.

"We'll talk about that later. Right now, fill me in," his boss demanded, all business, the subject of Stone and Soph off the table for the moment.

"Hagar showed his face yesterday. We're attempting to draw him out today. Soph is here with the woman who is in charge of housekeeping at the lodge. Jack's within reach while I'm backup."

"Do we have a sighting today?"

"No."

Ford frowned. "So we're still running blind?"

Stone hated to admit they didn't have a clue where Hagar was or where he'd been holed up, but the situation called for nothing except the truth. "Blind as a bat."

Ford nodded. "Chip and Aiden are mingling. We'll have more luck with the increase in eyes."

"Stone! She's gone. I can't find her. I've got Alice and Sadie. Neither of them know where Sophie is."

"What?" Stone pressed a hand to his ear. "Are you shitting me? How could they not know? They were all together!"

"We're moving toward the exit. Meet us there."

Stone was already heading around the back of the tent, Ford on his heels, barking orders into his phone.

"What the fuck happened, Jack?" Stone growled as he quickened his stride, his eyes glued to where Jack should be coming out of the tent.

The one Soph should have come out.

"Don't know. When I got through to the next section, Alice was calling out to Sophie. Sadie had gone ahead to see if she'd moved on without them. We're all coming out now."

Stone spotted Jack, Sadie, and Alice the second they cleared the canvas flap that blocked the exit and jogged to meet them.

"I don't understand, she was right there, then she was gone," Alice was saying to Jack while Sadie nodded.

"She was there, then not. It was so weird."

"Alice. Sadie. Did you hear her scream or call out?" Stone demanded as he stopped in front of them.

The older woman looked at him, shook her head. "No. There was so much noise in there but she never uttered a word. We were laughing one second and she was gone the next."

"We need to shut down the house. Start the search here," Ford barked behind him. "I'm bringing in the local law on this. Screw what her manager wants. My gut tells me this isn't a woman lost in a haunted house. This is a snatch."

Stone turned to look at his boss. "No. I—"

Ford held up his hand. "Do *what* I tell you, *when* I tell you, or I'm locking you down."

Instead of reprimanding him, Ford's words gave Stone a sense of relief. With fear eating at his insides, he couldn't think beyond what Hagar might be doing to Soph.

Every instinct told him his boss was right. The fucker had her. And he'd been the one to let her talk him into putting her at risk and his worst nightmare had come true.

He'd known. From the second he'd agreed to Jack and Soph's plan, he'd known the situation wasn't under their control.

Too many variables.

Too many places where their surveillance would be compromised.

Too many chances for Hagar to get close to Soph.

Anger and fear rose up inside him until he vibrated with energy. Before he registered what he was doing, he'd formed a fist and slammed it into Jack's stomach.

Ford's arms banded around Stone as Jack doubled over.

"You let him take her!" he yelled.

Jack straightened. "I'm giving you that one as a freebie."

He eyed his colleague, his friend, and struggled against the urge to punch him again.

"Take a breath, Stone. You're no good to her if you panic, if you lose control," Ford said in his ear.

"Fuck!" He broke out of his boss's hold and paced away. Ran both hands over his head and pulled at his hair. "We have to find her."

"We will." Jack moved beside him. "This fucker got her on my watch. Don't think that doesn't grind at me. We'll find her. We'll find *him*. And when we do, the fucker is going down."

"Hard." Stone took a deep breath and held it for a second. "The motherfucker is going down hard."

CHAPTER 17

Sophie stepped forward into the man who had hold of her sending him stumbling back, then quickly threw her weight in the opposite direction and wrenched her arm out of the hand gripping her elbow and darted back the way they'd come.

Except this section was really dark, darker than the others she'd walked through and she knew she'd been dragged away from Alice and Sadie before she'd realized what was going on and managed to break free.

Now she didn't know which way to go.

Luckily she could tell the difference between real life and a recording. She followed the sound of people laughing and screaming, of feet shuffling on the floor.

Slipping back into the crowd, she positioned herself in the middle of a group of older women.

They were laughing and mock screaming and didn't seem to notice she'd wiggled her way to the center of their group. She wasn't sure if she should continue with them or head back through the maze of ice walls to the entrance.

Turning, she took a step only to be pulled up short when an arm wrapped around her waist. Her muscles tensed and braced, ready to break away when someone whispered in her ear.

"Stick with us. We'll get you to the end and outside. We won't let that man grab you again."

Sophie's gaze met the older woman next to her. "I—"

She patted Sophie's arm with her free hand, the arm around her middle tightening and tugging her closer. "Don't worry. We've got you. We'll have you in the arms of your beau in no time."

"How—?"

Arm now linked with Sophie's, the woman winked and urged her forward. "We saw you yesterday on the Ferris wheel. I must admit I was surprised to see you here with Alice and Sadie and not that strapping young man again."

"But then we spotted him. And the other one. Knew something was going on." The woman on her right moved in, slipped her arm through Sophie's effectively sand-wiching her between the two of them. "Then that creep grabbed you. Two of the girls have gone after him."

"What? No." Sophie tried to turn back. "They can't."

"Oh, don't worry. They've got their bear spray handy."

"Bear spray?" Sophie wasn't sure what bear spray would do.

"Of course, dear, we all carry it. Not that anyone has actually seen a bear in town in years in spite of what old man Yancy says—everyone knows the man has a little too much Melt in his coffee, but you never know and it's always best to be safe than sorry."

"I—" Sophie blinked as the group pushed through a heavy flap of canvas out into the fresh air and sunshine.

"Soph!"

All air rushed from her lungs when two strong arms banded around her and lifted her off her feet. Her face was smushed into a warm neck by a hand cradling the back of her head and it only took one breath to know who held her.

"Stone." She breathed him in, wrapped her arms around his waist, and gripped fistfuls of his shirt.

"Della, what happened?" Alice asked from somewhere behind Stone. Sophie was too relieved to be in Stone's arms to lift her head and check on her new friend.

"Some guy tried to grab Sophie." A warm hand patted her shoulder. "We weren't going to let that happen."

"We?" Stone's chest vibrated against hers. "Who's we?"

"Me and the rest of the yarn crew."

"The yarn crew?" Stone asked.

"Yep. The Have-a-yarn crew get together every week to talk and sew or knit or crochet. Have done for going on thirty years now."

Sophie lifted her head to see Alice shaking hers, an indulgent smile on her face. "I should have known you wouldn't have gone in there without the whole crew but where are the others?" she asked.

"Inside trying to catch the guy."

"They're what?" a voice boomed.

She knew that voice; she might have only met him once

and talked on the phone once, but Ford Moreland had a distinctive voice. And he was standing about two feet away, an angry scowl on his face.

"Oh, don't worry, they're armed," the woman who had escorted her from the ice house assured him with a pat that turned into a stroke on Ford's chest.

"Armed?" Stone choked out.

"Jesus," Jack muttered.

"Someone save me from small town USA," Ford muttered. "Is that a good idea?" he asked the woman still stroking his chest.

She quickly dropped her hand from Ford and slammed it and her other one on her hips, an offended glare on her face. "Of course it is. They're armed with bear spray."

Ford sputtered, his mouth opening and closing, no words coming out.

"Don't you worry, young man. We're prepared to take on a black bear." The woman straighten to her full five-feet-four well rounded height. "One short man—a cowardly one at that—doesn't scare us."

"Black bear?" Ford looked at Sophie and she could clearly read the question in his eyes. *What the hell?* It was the same thought she had.

Before the conversation could go off track, Sophie turned to Stone. "Put me down."

"Not on promise of death right now, Soph. I need another minute here."

Sophie smiled, her gaze glued to his. "I promise you can still hold me, just put me down so I can turn around and say thank you. Please."

Stone's arms tightened for a second then eased her to the ground. "Don't leave my arms."

"Not on promise of death." Grinning she popped up on her toes and smacked her lips to his in a quick kiss. "Thanks."

"You scared the life out of me," he muttered.

Her smile vanished. "Me too, and I want nothing more than to stay wrapped up by you but we have to do this now."

With a nod, he let her go just enough that she could turn around. When she did, his arms went right back around her, tugging her tight against his chest.

When she faced everyone, Sophie took a deep breath. "I couldn't see much because it was dark. But the person who grabbed me was male, about five feet ten with a slender build. Short hair. No facial hair. He wore gloves and smelled like sawdust and some weird chemical odor I've never smelled before."

Ford stepped closer. "Do you think it was Hagar?"

"Yes. It had to be. Because if it wasn't, I'm the victim of a random attack or I've got two stalkers and either of those options would totally suck."

"Oh! Here comes the rest of the crew now." The woman who Sophie assumed was the ringleader rushed toward a group of women coming out of the ice house tent. "Where is he?" she demanded.

Looking flushed and very pissed off, a tall string-bean of a woman in a blue velour tracksuit with a white stripe down each side put her hands on her hips and all but spat out,

"Fucker got away. Thought we had him for a second but it turned out to be that young punk from the other side of the lake, Jeremy Sturgis, trying to cop a feel of anything with boobs. We showed him the results of that activity."

"Dammit. Did you at least get a good look at him, Bea?"

"Nope, sorry, Della. The bastard was in black, head to toe, including his face," Bea replied. "Knew what he was doing, that's for sure."

"Well," Della huffed. Turning back to Sophie she said, "I apologize. We weren't expecting to have to chase anyone."

"Please don't apologize, you were a huge help." Sophie assured her. If Della hadn't kept her with the group, who knows what Hagar might have managed to do.

"Wish we could have done more. Next time we'll—"

"There won't be a next time!"

Sophie slipped her hands over Stone's where they rested in tight fists on her stomach. "I appreciate you looking out for me but please, don't get into trouble or hurt on my account."

"Nonsense. We haven't had this much fun in ages, have we, ladies?"

Nods and words of agreement from the whole group had Sophie smiling.

"Well, I'm glad you thought this was fun. Unfortunately it's not. It's a very serious situation." Ford eyed each of the women in turn, and Sophie was sure his glare was meant to intimidate but none of the women seemed to bat an eye. "I thank you for your help today and hope I won't have to thank you again."

"You just do your job and catch the guy," Della said with a wave at Ford, Jack, and Stone. "Don't think we don't know why you're here."

"I'm just the boyfriend," Stone argued.

"Bear poo. You might be the boyfriend but that isn't all. Alice, I'll see you at the lodge later for our baking session?"

"Oh, yes, I've got everything ready to go."

"Baking session?" Sophie asked.

"We're baking the cookies and cupcakes for tomorrow afternoon," Alice said.

"What's on tomorrow afternoon?" Sophie had discovered each day of the festival had one major event.

Monday night had been the dance auction, yesterday had been the results of the 'local artist of the year' contest and today was the haunted ice house.

"Kids day. There will be races and games in the morning followed by a picnic lunch with cookies and cupcakes for dessert," Alice explained. "You can help if you want."

"I'd love to!" Sophie looked up at Stone. "Can I?"

"You're doing this at the lodge?" Stone asked Alice.

"Yes. In the main kitchen."

"Might be a good idea to get Sophie out of sight for a while," Ford added.

"We could use the time to strategize," Jack said.

"We could." Ford started tapping on his phone. "I'll get Aiden and Chip to meet us there."

CHAPTER 18

SOPHIE GLANCED AROUND AND SMILED.

She'd been smiling or laughing since the yarn crew arrived fifteen minutes ago. The women were a hoot.

Currently Della and Bea were arguing over how to hold a bag of flour correctly. They tugged the bag back and forth, each determined to prove she was right.

The bag slipped free and landed on the floor with a mushroom cloud of white powder that coated both women from shins to boobs. It didn't get any higher on account of them being so close after grappling over the bag.

Laughing, Sophie eyed the two women from the ground up.

Bea's blue and white velour suit was now completely white in front and when Della turned around, Sophie could see her emerald green dress had received the same makeover.

When she got to their faces, the looks they wore made Sophie laugh harder.

"Well," Della said with a mock frown and a poke to Sophie's middle. "I'm glad we could entertain you. But now we have a problem. We're short one bag of flour."

"I've got some in the staff kitchen," Alice said. "I'll get it when I bring the rest of the ingredients over."

Sophie and Alice had already carted a few bags of ingredients each from the staff wing to the Lodge's main kitchen before the other women had arrived but there was more that needed to be brought over. "I'll help you with those."

"Nonsense, it's only a few more things and you've already helped enough. I promised you a lesson in cookies and cupcakes and that doesn't include lugging stuff around." Alice made a shooing motion with her hand. "Why don't you give those two a hand cleaning up so we can get started when I get back?"

"If you're sure. I don't mind coming with you though."

"I know, dear, and I appreciate it but I'm going to see if I can get one of those strapping young men of yours to help me." Alice tipped her head to indicate the group of men in the far corner of the big industrial kitchen.

Sophie glanced over at the four men to find Stone's eyes on her.

It had been the same since they'd arrived back at the lodge from the festival. Every time she turned around he was either right beside her or watching her.

It should creep her out. Having Hagar watching her

every move certainly did. Except when it was Stone doing the looking, it felt different.

Completely different.

She didn't shiver because her skin crawled and she wanted to run and hide. She shivered because she wanted to strip naked and have his eyes on every inch of her bare skin.

The women had taken to calling them 'Sophie's men' but she only wanted one of them to be hers.

After his reaction to the incident in the ice house, Sophie thought maybe he could be hers when this was all over. Maybe, if she was lucky, Stone wouldn't walk away when it was no longer his job to keep her safe.

She'd promised herself—and him—last night that tomorrow would take care of itself, that she didn't want more than one night, except she'd lied.

She wanted him every night. For the rest of her life.

The squabbling yarn crew brought her out of her thoughts and she focused her gaze back on Stone. The frown told her he was reading her again.

He'd proven extremely efficient in his ability to gauge her moods and thoughts.

Smiling, she gave him a little finger wave and got back to the women surrounding her.

"Okay, let's get you two cleaned up and this mess off the floor so you can show me the best way to make cookies and cupcakes," she said as she headed toward the store-room she thought she'd find a broom in.

Alice had given her a quick tour of the kitchen when

they'd first walked in with armloads of ingredients so while she wouldn't say she knew her way around, she certainly wasn't clueless.

She'd been surprised when Alice had told her the lodge staff only used half the huge space nowadays. The lodge had to have over five hundred rooms and from what she knew, they were all booked due to the Ice Breaker Festival.

Surely that many people staying here required more staff and food prep than was being utilized. It didn't make sense.

She wasn't sure what to think about the lodge. In most of the areas Sophie had seen, it needed some TLC.

Alice had hinted at the General Manager not being interested in improving things and the owner was taking care of some personal issues and didn't pay as much attention to the place as he once had.

It seemed a shame to let the grand old building deteriorate. Not that she'd seen all that much of it.

Stone had kept her on lock down most of the time and when they had ventured out of their room, it had been to go into town.

She made a mental note to check out more of the lodge once they got this stalker thing out of the way.

Sophie grinned. Maybe she could convince Stone to spend some time with her here before they headed back to Australia when they'd dealt with the Hagar issue.

She had no doubt they would deal with Hagar. She'd been confident in Stone's ability to catch Hagar before Jack, and now Ford and the rest of the Landlocked team, had arrived.

Opening the door to the storeroom, Sophie searched for a light switch. Flicking it on, she spotted the broom hanging on the wall and had taken three steps towards it when the light went out.

Startled, she shot a hand out to grab a shelf just as a screech burst through the air. Two seconds later water poured down from the ceiling, drenching her in less than a second.

"What the hell?" Spinning around, she tried to make it back to the door, arms out in front of her. She'd only moved a step when someone bumped into her hands. "Stone—"

It wasn't Stone.

She knew that before she'd finished saying his name. She opened her mouth to scream but didn't get a sound out before a gloved hand covered her mouth and nose.

The chemical smell from earlier filled her nose. Made her eyes water.

She tried to jerk away but something held her in place and everything seemed to go in slow motion. Her limbs wouldn't work right and she could swear she was seeing things.

Some weird alien monster stood in front of her, its face distorted by an unearthly yellow glow.

Sophie knew she was in trouble, knew she needed to run or yell or something, anything, except nothing made sense.

Where was she?

Was she in the haunted ice house?

"It's fine. I've got you, Sophie."

Yes. Yes. It was fine.

Stone had her.

He'd protect her, keep her safe.

He'd always keep her safe.

He'd promised.

CHAPTER 19

THE LIGHTS WENT out a second before a piercing wail punched through his eardrums and the heavens opened. Except he wasn't outside.

They were in the kitchen at the lodge. And the fire alarm had been triggered.

Stone was already on the move, heading in the direction of Soph.

"What the fuck?" Ford yelled behind him.

"It's the fucking fire alarm. We're in the damn kitchen and there was nothing on fire before the bloody thing went off," Aiden yelled. "Where the fuck is Sophie?"

Stone moved faster. He knew what the hell this was. And it wasn't a fucking fire. "Someone get some lights on!"

He bumped a counter, heard things rattling and falling and didn't care, kept moving. He had to get to Soph before Hagar did. He should have stuck to her. Glued himself to her side instead of being across the room.

They hadn't checked the storerooms off the kitchen. They should have. They'd fucked up there. Big time.

If Hagar hurt one hair on Soph's head, Stone would kill the man. And never forgive himself for letting it happen.

Chaos rained around him. Water burst from the sprinklers drenching everything, women gasped and squealed, and his Landlocked colleagues yelled orders behind him.

It was a testament to their team that Jack followed behind him while the rest of them tried to calm the women and gain control of the situation.

Stone kicked open the storeroom door; a beam of light cut through the dark over his shoulder and revealed an empty room. Not empty but not containing the one thing he was looking for.

"Soph!" He knew it was futile, knew she wasn't here without checking every corner of a room that had no real corners to hide in. "Fuck!"

Jack moved in beside him, swung his torch over every surface to no avail. Soph was gone.

"Motherfucker," Jack cursed.

"I'm killing him."

"I'll help you bury the body."

As one they spun around and with only the light from Jack's torch, moved on to the next storeroom. Again, they found no Soph.

"Dammit. We need to get outside," Stone said, already heading for the door.

Sirens and panicked people met them when they left the lodge through the emergency exit.

Lights flashed and uniformed men yelled. The chaos outside tripled what had surrounded them in the kitchen.

"Jesus, we've got no hope of finding anyone in this mob," Jack muttered.

Glancing at his friend, Stone tried to swallow the lump in his throat he was pretty sure was his heart before murmuring, "We have to find her."

Jack clapped him on the shoulder. "We will. It might not be in the next few minutes but we'll find her," Jack vowed.

Ford charged toward them. "We're going to have to coordinate with the locals."

"I thought her manager wanted this on the down low?" Jack asked.

Stone's stomach tightened. "I don't care who knows. In fact I want everyone to know. The quickest way to catch this guy now is to go public. He's been here as long as Soph and we still don't know where he's been hiding. The best way to find out who's where in this place is to get the locals on it. Where's the yarn crew? They should be our first stop."

"Already spreading the word," Ford answered. "I only left them to find you two and then head for the police chief." Ford tipped his head in the direction of the man who was clearly in charge of all the uniforms on scene.

Stone nodded. "I'll scout the perimeter. Once they get the alarm and sprinklers off if we haven't found Soph, we'll comb the inside for clues."

"Go. Jack take his six."

He didn't wait for any further instructions, he took off

in the direction of the parking lot. Hagar would need a way out of here. A car was the obvious choice.

By the time he and Jack had searched the front area of the lodge and moved to the back side, the one butting up against the lake, Stone knew they'd fucked up again.

Hagar hadn't taken Soph out of there by car.

He'd gone by boat.

CHAPTER 20

Sophie's head hurt and her stomach churned. Moaning, she rolled to the side, her hands flying to her head as it spun to match her belly.

Swallowing the bile rising up her throat, she licked her dry lips and retched at the foul taste that coated them.

Fighting to keep from throwing up, she squeezed her eyes tight and tried to remember what the hell she'd done last night.

She hadn't had a hangover this bad in years.

Stomach somewhat under control, she took a deep breath and let it out slowly. When that didn't bring about the threat of vomiting, she drew in another one. And another. Feeling steadier, she decided to brave moving again.

With great effort, she cracked her eyelids and tried to focus. Her vision was blurred but even that didn't disguise the dirt beneath her.

Where the bloody hell was she?

Looking up, she took in the wood wall opposite and raked her memories for some kind of recognition.

The timber boards were grayed, the gaps between them widened with age. Neither of which triggered a memory.

Deep silence surrounded her. Nothing moved. Nothing breathed and the dead quiet—and her steadier belly—gave her the courage to turn her head and look around more.

She pushed up to her hands and knees and rode out the woozy sensation that followed. Using the wall beside her, she climbed to her feet.

Her head pounded.

"Bloody hell," she whispered, setting off another beat inside her skull.

Her throat felt tight, raw, as though she'd spent hours and hours singing. But she couldn't recall doing a concert or being in the studio.

Other than her aching head, tumbling stomach, and sore throat, she seemed unharmed.

Well, as unharmed as having a blank memory made her.

Had she been in an accident? Hit her head?

With her head still spinning, the possibility of being in an accident seemed plausible. It also made it difficult to concentrate.

The last thing she remembered was... Being in a kitchen. Flour everywhere. Laughing at—

OMG! The yarn crew! Stone!

Head whipping around, eyes wide, Sophie lost her balance. Crashing to the ground, she cried out as pain stabbed through her hip.

Crumpled on the dirt, she panted and whimpered, focused on getting her breathing even, her stomach still.

When the nausea and dizziness finally passed, Sophie rolled over and eased into a sitting position against the wall behind her. Supported, she glanced around the cavernous building and discovered she was definitely alone.

Wherever she was, and it appeared to be some sort of abandoned building; it hadn't been frequented by people or animals in a long, long time.

Dirt and dust lay in piles where she imagined the breeze blew through the cracks in the walls. Sun streamed in through holes in the roof above her and the large doors at the far end of the building sat crooked on their rusty hinges.

The place was a death trap, waiting to collapse at the first strong wind or go up in flames at the drop of a match.

Regardless of the fact she still had no idea where she was or how she'd gotten here, she had to get out.

Waiting around wasn't her style. It was how she'd ended up in the States, why she'd finally had enough of the madman following her...

She sucked in a breath and choked on the dust in the air.

Hagar.

Her gaze zipped around, searching for any sign of the man who'd followed her for weeks. The man she was one hundred percent certain was the reason she was here.

The creak of wood and the scrape of metal had her focusing on the doors meters away. With dread, Sophie watched, air stuck in her lungs, blocked by her heart pounding triple time in her throat.

He came through the small gap he'd made, the welcoming smile and tray of food doing nothing to extinguish her fear.

"Oh good, you're awake. I was starting to worry I'd given you too much Rohypnol."

"Bloody hell." He'd drugged her. No wonder she couldn't remember what the hell happened.

A shudder of revulsion ripped through her. What had he done to her while she was under the influence of the date-rape drug?

"I brought you some food. I wanted to make your favorite but the kitchen in the old house doesn't work so I'm using a camp stove which isn't the best," he babbled as he drew closer. "I wish I could offer you a shower to go with the clean clothes I bought for you but there's no running water here either. I promise to stop at a hotel as soon as we can so you can freshen up."

Sophie wasn't sure how to take this guy. He seemed harmless until she looked at those weird eyes.

She'd never seen a color like them before and wondered if they were real or contacts. Although the crazy lurking in them was definitely real.

"Here." He put the tray down in front of her. "Eat up and I'll get our things together so we can leave."

"Leave?"

He smiled, the turn of his lips creepy in combination with his ice blue eyes. "Yes. We need to get going or we'll miss our plane home."

"Home?"

"Of course. You didn't think we would stay here, did you?" He glanced around them. "I'm not opposed to living in the mountains but I've got us a nice beach house on the coast of northern Queensland. Eat up. We've got a long trip ahead of us."

She didn't want to go anywhere with him. He'd drugged her, taken her, dumped her in this abandoned building, and acted as though he cared?

Her head might still be spinning from the drug but she wasn't stupid enough to go with him. She just had to find the right moment to get away.

"Eat, eat," he said from the crooked door. "I'll be back soon."

Eyeing the sandwich and glass of water he'd put in front of her, Sophie contemplated the odds he'd drugged them.

She was a little dehydrated but didn't want to risk ingesting more of the sedative he'd used and she didn't feel hungry so she pushed the tray away and waited for her kidnapper to return.

CHAPTER 21

Sophie didn't wait long. Hagar returned carrying a plastic bag, his smile quickly turning to a frown when he noticed she hadn't touched the food.

"You haven't eaten. We don't have time. You need to eat."

He seemed a little agitated and she tried to placate him. "I'm feeling a bit sick. Can I take it with me?"

"Oh. Sorry. I don't want you to feel sick. Didn't want to hurt you but I needed to get you away from those men. They don't know how to take care of you the way I do." He smiled, his eyes dipping to her wrist. "I'm glad you liked the bracelet I made you."

She looked at the charm bracelet a fan had sent her in the mail and the cute charms turned sinister. "Y-you made this?"

"Yes. Yes." He grinned and she was reminded of the

young kids that came to her concerts. "It has a special charm, see?"

Sophie couldn't stop herself from flinching when he reached down and pointed to the little silver house but he didn't seem to notice her aversion to his touch.

"I put something special inside there. It helps me know where you are all the time."

Oh god. He'd tagged her! Like a bloody dog!

She wanted to rip the damn thing off. Throw it across the room. But she didn't dare. Hagar might seem harmless on the surface but she'd learned he wasn't without his resources to get her where he wanted her.

For now her best option was to go along with him and wait for the right moment to overpower him or escape.

"Um, I need to use a bathroom." She didn't, except the necessity might get her out of this building quicker than he'd planned. The more she kept him off kilter, the better her chances of getting away.

"Oh. Yes. Yes. Silly me. You should change in the house. The toilet doesn't flush but you can still use it."

"Is it far?"

"No. Just through the trees." He picked up the tray. "I'll wrap your lunch while you change, then we can leave."

Pushing to her feet, Sophie found herself steady, the lingering nausea and dizziness minimal. She kept quiet when he led her from the building and through a small group of trees.

An old house came into view and she instantly knew why the toilet didn't work.

Sagging roof, broken windows, some boarded up, and holes in the outer walls told their own story.

"Right in here." Hagar held the back door open. "The bathroom is through there."

She couldn't understand why he was so trusting but she wasn't about to ponder it and instead headed to the bathroom.

"Here. Don't forget your clothes."

Turning, she found him holding out the plastic bag.

Forcing a smile she said, "Thanks," took the bag, and rushed as fast as she could to the bathroom.

Locked behind the door, Sophie's mind raced with ways to get out of there without having to go with Hagar.

Glancing in the bag, she found an ugly grey shift dress in a size too big for her and a pair of shoes that she'd never be seen dead in.

Chucking them aside, she looked in the cracked mirror and decided other than being dirty she'd do the way she was.

Besides, she didn't want to wear anything that was from him. Starting with the stupid bracelet.

Tugging on the clasp, she grunted in frustration when the tiny clip took forever to open. Disgusted she'd worn it for weeks, she dropped it on the pile of clothes and scanned the room for a way out.

The window was too small to fit through and there wasn't any other exit except the way she'd entered. Taking a deep breath she squared her shoulders and opened the door.

Silence greeted her.

Had he left?

Stepping into the hall, she decided to explore the house and if Hagar found her she'd pretend she'd been looking for him.

The living room proved empty except for an old armchair in one corner. Nothing she could use as a weapon.

Two bedrooms, also barren of anything but dust gave her no hope of freedom either.

It was the third, and what she assumed was the master bedroom at the front of the house, which delivered the first glimpse of possible escape.

Leaning against the wall in the back of the closet was a shotgun.

With no clue how to use it, she grabbed the weapon as the back door slammed.

"Sophie, honey, are you ready?"

A shudder rattled her teeth and her stomach rolled. "Bloody hell," she muttered. "He's a complete nut-job."

"There you are." He stepped behind her. Too close. "What have you found?"

Sophie scrambled to remember the moves Stone had taught her.

Soft spots.

Groin, eyes, throat, nose…

He reached past her. "Give me—"

She sank her teeth into his arm.

"Ouch!"

Spinning around she kicked up and hit him square in the balls with her wedge heel.

As he bent over cupping his groin, she swung the gun and smashed the thick barrel across his face.

Blood sprayed out and he yelped in pain before he dropped to the floor at her feet.

CHAPTER 22

Stone was going out of his mind and pretty sure he was driving everyone around him insane while he was at it.

"Where the fuck is she?"

Nobody answered.

Then again, no one had the million-and-one other times he'd muttered the same question in the last twelve hours, so it seemed unlikely they would now.

"We might have a lead."

He spun around and stared at the local cop, deputy, sheriff, whatever the hell they called themselves. He didn't give a rat's ass as long as they helped him find Soph. "What?"

"A group of high school kids were hanging out around the back of the Bar and Grill—"

"Where?" Stone had no idea what that was, never mind where.

"The restaurant bar at the lodge," the officer clarified.

"The lodge? Winter Lake Lodge?" He needed to be clear on where this guy was talking about.

"Yes." Chief Yunker, according to the guy's badge, motioned a teenager forward. "Tell them what you saw, Hammond."

"A fireman carrying a woman over his shoulder climbed out one of the windows at the back of the lodge. Pretty sure it was the women's restroom next to the bar where Kennedy works."

"Kennedy? Carrying?" Stone asked.

"My sister. I was waiting for her to get off work." The boy shrugged. "The woman looked asleep or unconscious. She was all floppy."

"Was she injured?" Stone asked the boy. If she was out cold...

He shook his head. "Didn't look like it. There wasn't any blood or anything."

"He must have drugged her." Jack moved next to him, speaking the thought running through Stone's mind. "Makes sense when you think about it. No way Sophie would go with him without a fight."

"He had to have injected her with something." Stone could see it playing out in his head.

Hagar had to have been waiting for her, following her, until he found the perfect moment to grab her.

The fact the boy said it was a fireman meant Hagar had been in disguise. Again. It explained why they hadn't spotted him.

None of them would have looked twice at a fireman

when searching the crowd after the false alarm. Then again, Hagar would have been long gone before then.

"With all the noise and darkness after the lights went out and the alarm went off, it's unlikely she would have noticed him coming at her with a syringe," Chip speculated. "Then again he may have just had chloroform on a cloth, come up behind her, covered her mouth and nose..."

Both scenarios made sense.

"And just because she wasn't bleeding doesn't mean he didn't hit her over the head," Aiden added.

Stone clenched his fists as he turned to Ford and asked, "Have we got anything else?"

It was Chief Yunker who answered him. "The station took a call yesterday morning from Mrs. Brindle about some suspicious activity around the old Horsham place over in Broken Bay. We sent a car out there but the officer didn't see anything or anyone around. I figured we should take a closer look. Besides the old homestead, there are a few barns and machine sheds that could be used to hide something or someone."

"The guy didn't check all the buildings?" Ford asked.

"Didn't see a reason too. There was nothing to indicate recent activity."

Damn sleepy little towns and their lack of urgency. Stone had to admit that thought was unfair; even in a big city the police might not have investigated further, under those circumstances.

Soph hadn't been missing when the call came in, and they'd deliberately kept the local authorities in the dark about her stalker.

"Then let's get out there and take a closer look," Stone demanded.

"We already did."

"You went without telling me?" Ford asked.

"No offense, Mr. Moreland, but in spite of your skills and your company's employment as Ms. Collins's personal protection, you have no authority here. This is a potential kidnapping, which is a crime our department takes seriously. I personally led the search undertaken not an hour ago. There was no sign of Ms. Collins or her possible abductor."

"I understand your position, and I'll respect that we *might* have overstepped a few lines by being here without your knowledge. But this concerns two Australian citizens, one of whom is a criminal *without* the added charge of abduction. With the skills my men collectively have, I'm sure you can see why combining our resources would be in the best interests of all. Particularly in regard to the safe return of Sophie Collins," Ford challenged.

Stone stood back and let his boss debate the merits of joining forces with the local cops. He definitely couldn't be diplomatic about things in his current mental state of raw panic, and he couldn't risk being shut out of the search altogether—which Ford had threatened to do after he'd punched Jack in the gut and again right after Soph had gone missing last night.

Another local uniform rushed into the room and headed straight for the one now in a heated discussion with Ford. "Chief." The newcomer addressed his colleague but glanced in Stone's direction.

Yunker turned. "Scott. What have you got?"

"We've had a report of a man walking down the highway from Broken Bay."

"And this is of interest in the disappearance of Sophie Collins?" Yunker asked with a frown.

Scott's mouth tipped up in a grin. "He's being *forced* to walk toward town by a woman wielding a gun, according to the witness who called it in."

"A gun?"

Scott nodded. "And he's naked."

Jack snorted behind him and Stone didn't bother to hide his own smile as he asked, "What's the woman with the gun wearing?"

"Her clothing matches the description of what Sophie Collins was wearing when she disappeared."

"Have we got a car headed out there?" Yunker asked.

"We have one on scene now. She refused assistance. In fact, she threatened to shoot Laura if she tried to arrest her 'prisoner'."

Stone couldn't hold back a chuckle and Jack was outright laughing now.

"Wait," Ford interrupted. "Are you actually saying Sophie Collins managed to get free and has in fact taken her stalker *hostage* and is in the process of bringing him into town?"

"Yes, sir. Although she refused to give her name to Laura, the woman matches the photo we circulated; Laura has no doubt the two people walking in front of her cruiser are Sophie Collins and George Hagar," Scott answered.

"This I have to see." Ford headed for the door.

Stone stopped Scott when he turned to follow the others. "Is Soph okay?" he asked.

"Physically? I think so. Laura said other than being dirty and stubborn, she appeared in good health, which is why I told her to back off and follow," Scott explained.

Relief flowed through him. If she was able to argue, Hagar couldn't have hurt her badly. "How far out are they?"

"Laura said five minutes, max. Ms. Collins is making her kidnapper walk fast."

"And she doesn't want him cuffed and in the car?"

"Oh no, he's cuffed. But she refuses to allow him the luxury of hiding in a car. Said something about needing to teach him a lesson in vulnerability and exposure."

Stone smiled. He could understand Soph's reasoning. Hagar had stripped her of her defenses and left her vulnerable and in fear for weeks. It seemed fair she return the favor.

"You coming?" Jack asked from the door.

"Yep."

Although now that he knew Soph was okay he didn't feel the urgency of the last twelve hours.

The longer they took to get to her, the longer she got to mete out her own brand of justice.

CHAPTER 23

Sophie couldn't wait to get out of the sun and have a cold drink. The warm water she'd found in Hagar's stash of supplies had done little to alleviate her thirst and the hour walk in the mid-morning sun hadn't helped at all either.

She'd almost given in and let the police officer take them to town, but she'd come this far, and even with the miles she'd forced Hagar to walk naked, he hadn't suffered enough.

No. She wanted him to have to walk through the middle of town, where all the people attending the festival could get an eyeful.

At first she'd made him strip just because she could. The fear he'd obviously felt when he'd come to and discovered she'd turned the tables and held a gun on him hadn't been enough for her.

She needed him stripped bare, and it made sense to take his clothes, to remove that outer protection.

Her desire for revenge took her by surprise. She'd never been deliberately mean to anyone before.

Maybe this whole stalker experience had strengthened her spine, because she wasn't going to be putting up with other people's bad treatment any longer.

Sophie was going to stop letting people take advantage of her.

Starting with her parents.

Sophie's parents had only ever been interested in the money she could give them—that she 'owed' them—and even though they obviously weren't on the same level as Hagar, they had, in their own way, bullied her over the years.

She'd even allowed her manager to talk her into doing things she wasn't comfortable with.

Frowning, she recalled the last argument they'd had, the one she'd refused to lose.

She'd gone to Reginald about the strange man following her and he'd freaked out and wanted to get her twenty-four hour protection.

They'd argued for hours. She'd finally buckled and allowed him to have a security company install a new alarm system at her house and investigate the man she'd described.

Then again look where she'd ended up. Maybe she owed Reginald an apology for that argument.

Although it did seem as though she'd gotten out of this situation on her own in the end.

Though she couldn't deny the moves Stone had taught

her had saved her life. She'd done exactly as he'd shown her; hit the soft spots on a man's body he'd told her to hit.

She smiled when she remembered the way Hagar had groaned, his hands cupping his groin after she'd kicked him with all her might with her four-inch wedge heels.

The same heels now rubbing her feet raw. Perhaps she should have accepted a ride from Officer Murdock.

"Soph."

Her head snapped to the side, her gaze colliding with Stone's smiling hazel eyes.

"You still can't do as you're told, can you?"

"What?" She glanced around and noticed there were more men with Stone. Jack she recognized, as well as Ford Moreland. "Mr. Moreland."

He tipped his head. "Ms. Collins."

"I definitely remember saying you weren't getting your hands on a gun, Soph."

She bought her gaze back to Stone. "Well, no, you said I wasn't getting my hands on *your* gun, but this isn't yours, and to be honest, I think I can be forgiven for disregarding that particular instruction."

Stone nodded but other than his sparkling eyes, his expression remained serious. "Did he hurt you?"

Frowning, she looked over at Hagar. Someone had thrown a blanket around his shoulders. "Hey! He's still got to walk through town to the station."

"I understand why you want that to happen, Ms. Collins, but I'm afraid I have to object. There are a lot of children at the festival today and I'm sure you can appreciate the necessity of covering him up," the police officer standing beside Hagar said.

He wasn't the nice officer who'd spent the last few minutes following Sophie in her car, but he seemed as though he was really sorry to ruin her punishment for Hagar, and he *did* have a point.

"Oh." Frowning, she murmured, "I never thought of that."

"Soph." Stone had moved closer.

"What now?" she huffed in frustration. This wasn't the way she'd planned things, and really, she just needed a drink of water.

"Give me the gun." She stared at his outstretched hand then down at the weapon in hers.

"I wouldn't have shot him."

"I know."

"I wanted to."

"Understandable."

"I couldn't work out how to use it," she whispered.

Stone leaned in. "He doesn't know that, does he?" he whispered back.

She shook her head.

He laughed. Put his hand over hers and slipped the gun from her grip. "Come here."

Sophie didn't see him hand the weapon off but the next second she was wrapped in his arms and collapsing with relief and exhaustion.

"C'mon. Let's get you looked at." Lifting her as though she weighed nothing, Stone cradled her against his chest and walked to the car parked across the road.

"I'm okay," she murmured into his neck. "Just need a drink."

And sleep. She needed to sleep.

CHAPTER 24

Two months.

Two months, three days, and fifteen hours.

"But who's counting?" Stone mumbled.

He pulled into the driveway beside the tiny red convertible and sighed. She'd gone and bought the damn car.

With a smile, he hit the button to cut the engine and climbed out of his Cherokee. Soph wasn't the only one with new wheels.

He'd splurged on the limited edition when he'd left Landlocked and started his own company.

The offer had come out of the blue and Ford had told him if he didn't take it, he'd fire Stone's ass so he had no choice but to take the opportunity to branch out on his own.

He hadn't had the heart to tell Ford he'd had one foot out the door from the minute he'd landed back in Sydney two months ago.

But he'd needed to wait. To give Soph time to reevaluate and determine if what they'd shared was more than the intense situation they'd met under.

There was no question about his feelings. He was in love with Sophie Collins. She was all he thought about.

Every waking—and sleeping—moment was taken up with memories of her sparkling green eyes, her laughter, the taste of her on his tongue, the feel of her wrapped around—

Stone shook his head and chuckled. The woman had him tied in knots, his cock semi-erect twenty-four seven, and he hadn't had his hands on her in months—hadn't laid eyes on her.

"Are you coming in or what?"

Fuck. Her silky-smooth voice skipped over his skin in a trail of prickly heat. He turned to find her leaning against the frame of her open front door.

The sight of her took his breath. His eyes soaked her in. From head to toes, he catalogued the changes.

Her hair was longer, the thick brown waves almost brushing her waist now, and he couldn't wait to tangle his fingers in those soft strands and kiss her senseless.

Business first.

He'd have to suffer from the worst case of blue balls in history for a little while longer.

Smiling, he started up the path. "Did you get the papers I sent over?"

"Yes." She pushed off the doorjamb and shook her head. "But I'm not signing them."

He frowned. "Why not?"

"There are a few things I need answered before I sign with your security company."

What the fuck? *She'd* been the one to ask him to go out on his own so she could hire him. "Like?"

"Why don't we take this discussion inside?" Without waiting for an answer, Soph turned on her bare heel and walked into the house.

Following, Stone took no notice of his surroundings. He was too busy checking out her ass in the skin-tight jeans she wore. The material cupped her rear end the way his hands longed to.

"Stop perving on my butt, Stone."

He could hear the smile in her voice. "It's a great butt," he responded. There wasn't any point in denying the perving.

"Whatever." She led him into a living room filled with large comfy-looking leather couches and a huge screen covering the far wall. "Take a seat. I'll grab us a drink."

"I don't need a seat or a drink. I want to know why you won't sign the paperwork I had drawn up. You're the one who asked me to do this."

"Fine." Soph flopped onto a couch and smiled up at him. "Can you do the job I'm hiring you for and see me at the same time?"

"See you? Isn't that what the job requires? Seeing you

every day." His chest tightened, his heart racing with the implication of her words. Except he wasn't jumping to conclusions; he needed every detail spelled out.

"Are you being obtuse on purpose?"

"No."

"Then you know what I'm saying."

"I need it clearer."

"Fine, can you take care of my security needs and sleep in my bed with me?"

"Sleep in your bed?"

"I want you to move in with me."

"Wow." Shit. That was way more than he'd hoped for when he'd walked away all those weeks ago. Except... "Why? Why do you want me to move in here?"

She blew out a breath and looked up at the ceiling. "Anyone ever tell you you're a very frustrating man?"

"Sure. But that doesn't answer my question."

"Okay, how about this?" Soph brought her gaze to his. "I'm in love with you and I know you feel the same."

"Confident."

"Definitely. I respect that you thought we needed time to be sure our feelings weren't a product of the high-stakes situation that brought us together, but I'm done giving you time to be sure."

"Me?" he croaked.

She frowned. "Yes, you."

"It wasn't me who needed to be sure."

"Of course it was," she argued.

Stone chuckled. How could she be so oblivious? "I've known from the second I pulled you into my arms that first day. I might have fought it and tried to deny it, but it was a done deal from that moment."

"So you were giving *me* time?"

Stone nodded.

"Bloody hell. We've wasted weeks!"

He laughed.

"It's not funny! I've been going out of my bloody mind. I even had to throw out my phone charger so I *couldn't* call you."

Reaching down, he grabbed her hand and tugged her to her feet, pulling her against his chest. "Will you sign those papers now?"

She tilted her head and squinted at him. "I don't know... I'm not sure I like you anymore."

"Is this like the Ferris wheel?" He bent to nuzzle the soft skin of her throat. "I seem to remember you pretending you didn't like me then too."

"I want to go back."

Stone raised his head to look at her. "What?"

"To Winter Lake. I want to go back for the festival."

"It's over."

"Yes, but it's on every year."

"Okay."

"Easy as that?"

"I think we established when it comes to each other, we're both easy."

"A tough guy like you?"

Stone smiled. "When it comes to love, it's the tough guys who go down the hardest."

Sophie lay on the picnic rug and wiggled in closer to Stone.

"Warm enough?" he asked, his arm tightening around her waist.

"Hmm." She breathed in the spring air and smiled. "I'm so glad we're here."

"I promised we'd return."

She twisted her neck and looked up at Stone. "Thank you for bringing me back. I needed to see it without—"

He kissed her. Sweeping his tongue along the seam of her lips, he encouraged her to open for him. Like she could resist anything this man wanted.

In the last year, they'd definitely proven they were easy for each other. And he wasn't the only one who'd gone down hard.

"We're not talking about that ever again, remember?" he murmured against her lips.

She sighed when he tucked her securely into his side once more.

She'd never felt the depth of emotion she experienced with Stone. He was her everything. Twelve months ago, if someone had asked her what she feared losing the most, she'd have said her voice—her songs.

Now the answer would be Stone.

He was her rock. Her foundation. The reason for her existence.

Okay, that was probably a little dramatic, except Sophie couldn't deny she'd crumble into a million pieces if he ever left her.

Fear of that exact thing had been plaguing her for weeks now. He'd been distant—secretive—and she couldn't shake her unease. Couldn't help thinking maybe he wanted out of their relationship. That he was trying to find the right way to make the break. Their lives were so entwined now and he was responsible for overseeing all of her security needs.

"C'mon. Let's take one last ride on the Ferris wheel before the fireworks start."

He had them both on their feet in seconds. "But—"

"Alice will save our spot," Stone assured her while pulling her toward the ride.

"You go enjoy yourselves. We'll wait right here," Alice called out after them, her new grand baby snuggled in her arms.

"Stone." Sophie grunted when her shoe caught in a tuft of grass.

"Whoa." He scooped her against him. "I told you to ditch the heels."

"I'm not going barefoot. Who knows what's on the ground around here after someone let all those animals loose."

Light flashed. A second later the boom of the first firework rocked them and a kaleidoscope of color filled the sky.

"Shit. Missed it," Stone grumbled.

"Missed what?"

"Our chance to ride." Stone let her go and stepped back. "Soph," he said as he dropped to one knee.

"What are you doing? Get up. You don't know what's on the grass."

"My knee is on the grass, Soph." He smiled up at her as more light exploded overhead, the detonations vibrating through the air. "*One* knee."

"Yes, and I— Bloody hell. *Are you...?*"

Stone chuckled and shook his head. "Sophie Collins, for once in your life, zip it."

She rolled her lips between her teeth as her vision blurred.

"Right. Now, where was I?" He opened his palm, a small velvet box sitting in the center. He popped the lid up and Sophie couldn't stop the cry of delight that snuck up her throat. "Marry me."

"Yes!"

She launched herself at him. Taken completely by surprise, Stone couldn't stop them from tumbling to the ground in a tangle of arms and legs, and she didn't care what they were rolling around in. All she could think about was kissing him.

When they finally came up for air, they'd drawn a crowd, who were cheering and clapping.

"Bloody hell," she muttered and buried her tear-streaked face against Stone's chest. "I thought you were going to break up with me."

"What?" He rolled to the side, gripped her chin, and forced her to look at him. "Why on earth would you think that?"

"You've been acting funny. Secretive." She shrugged. "I thought…"

Stone laughed. "I told you the tough guys go down hard, Soph, but obviously I forgot to mention that I have no intention of getting up. I'm not letting you go—hence the ring you still aren't wearing."

"Oh." She scrambled to her knees and thrust out her left hand. "Here. Put it on."

He stayed on the ground while he retrieved the ring from its box. Slowly.

"Hurry up," she prompted.

"This ring comes with one condition."

"Anything." She wiggled her fingers. "Just put it on already."

"You haven't heard what I want yet."

"As long as you put that ring on my finger, I don't care."

"I want to get married here."

"Here?"

"This week."

"This week?!"

"The secret behavior you were worried about?"

She frowned. Nodded.

"I planned our wedding."

"You... Our... *Wedding?*" Her jaw worked but for some reason she couldn't find the right words to string together in a way that made sense. Probably because nothing Stone had said made sense to her.

"With the help of Alice and Sadie, I've arranged for us to be married in the town gazebo this Sunday."

"While the festival is still on?" She blinked. Her eyes stung as what he was telling her finally began to make sense.

"It seemed fitting. We met here," he continued but she was already sold on the idea. It was perfect for them.

"Oh my god, I love it. Yes! Let's do it here. On Sunday. Now put my ring on!" She reached for his hand but he moved it out of the way. "Hey. That's mine."

"And this is mine." Stone used his free arm to wrap around her waist and pull her down on top of him. "I love you."

"Bloody hell. Love you too. Now stop stalling and *put my ring on!*"

Laughing, he gripped her hand and made a huge production out of slipping the ring onto her finger.

Turning her hand around, she admired the emerald surrounded in diamonds and asked, "Why an emerald?"

"It matches your eyes, and it didn't feel right getting you the standard diamond solitaire. I wanted a unique ring for a unique woman." He smiled sheepishly.

Ah. He was so sweet. He'd obviously thought about it seriously. "Oh, we need to get you a ring."

"I bought the one that matches your wedding set but if you want to choose something different, we can look tomorrow."

She couldn't believe he'd considered all the details. "You've thought of everything."

He shrugged. "Not everything. I didn't plan for us to be rolling around in the grass when I proposed."

"You could have asked me in a pig pen. I'd have still said yes."

"A pig pen? You turning into a nature lover on me?"

"Oh hell no, but I'm not stupid. I'm not letting the chance to spend the rest of my life with you get away. When you love someone you'll do whatever it takes. Besides, we both know I'm easy-peasy when it comes to you."

If you enjoyed this book, please consider leaving a review. It only takes a few minutes and you'll be helping other readers find stories they'll enjoy, as well as supporting authors you love.

For what's coming next, latest releases, sales and more, join
Rhian's Royal Readers
http://www.rhiancahill.com/contact/newsletter/

ACKNOWLEDGMENTS

Fedora, I've apologized time and time again for pushing us to the line and this time I shoved us right over it but you still stuck with me and for that I'll be forever grateful.

Tamara I stole your last name. Hope you don't mind but then again, you kind of have no choice. ;)

If you've gotten this far THANK YOU! Thank you for choosing my book to read. Thank you for liking Sophie and Stone, and Winter Lake enough to make it to this point. Hope to see you in Winter Lake again soon.

xoxo
Rhian

ABOUT THE AUTHOR

Rhian Cahill is the alter ego of a former stay-at-home mother of four. With motherly duties rapidly dwindling, Rhian is able to make use of the fertile imagination she used to keep herself sane for all those years of slavery. Years spent living overseas and visiting tropical climates have helped inspire some steamy stories.

Multi-published in erotic romance, paranormal romance, and contemporary romance, Rhian, with the help of Mr. Muse, spends her days and nights writing.

When not glued to the keyboard you'll find her, book or knitting in hand, avoiding any and all housework as much as possible.

For more on Rhian –

Website – http://www.rhiancahill.com/
Newsletter signup – http://www.rhiancahill.com/contact/newsletter/
FaceBook – https://www.facebook.com/RhianCahillAuthor

Instagram – http://instagram.com/rhiancahill/

Twitter – https://twitter.com/RhianCahill

BookBub – https://www.bookbub.com/authors/rhian-cahill

Goodreads – https://www.goodreads.com/rhian_cahill

Does it really matter that she thinks she's going home with his buddy, Alec Dane?

Apparently it does because she sneaks away the morning after. *Twice.* First, when she discovers her mistake, then when she decides her upcoming move to Winter Lake makes them a two-day stand at best. But the sex is off-the-charts combustible, and Alex is already seeing stars, hearing bells...envisioning houses and picket fences and other things he'd never considered.

Now all he has to do is convince Sadie his feelings are real. His shy wallflower might consider him a mistake—but Alex has never been more certain.

Let Me Love You

He's got moves on — and off — *the field.*

As receiver for the Miami Storm, Grady Murdock couldn't be more satisfied with his professional life. Next up—his personal one. He's a player on the field, not off, so when he claps eyes on Melinda at a Storm event, he's neither surprised nor alarmed to find she triggers both lustful and long-term thoughts. Six years his senior, Mel isn't so easily convinced.

Independent, career-minded Melinda Shaw has singlehandedly built one of Miami's premier event-management companies, but success hasn't stopped her heart from shifting its focus to marriage and children. Still, she's not about to burden a younger man with her fantasies of familial grandeur...until she does.

Their combustible sexual chemistry notwithstanding, Grady still has to work overtime to convince Mel he wants her despite their impending parenthood, not because of it. It'll take almost losing everything—and more than a few of Grady's famous moves—to score Mel's heart once and for all.

Wild Rush Of Love

Drinks aren't the only thing this barman is serving up.

Tending bar at Winter Lake Lodge, Rush Whelan enjoys all the fun with the female clientele, with none of the commitment. They come for vacation—and for Rush, in his bed—then they go. Until Sabreena. After spending her entire holiday together, Rush still can't get the shy beauty out of his mind. When he finds himself with some unexpected time off, there's only one thing to do—follow Reena home.

Waitress Sabreena Howe is grateful for the built-in family that comes with working at Pat's Pub. Mr. Collins and his brood have taken in more than a few strays, Reena among them. But even with their support, Reena has trouble letting people get close... including Rush. Despite their instant connection, Reena allowed fear to abort what could have been their amazing last night together.

When Rush shows up in Baltimore, Reena finally sets her trepidation aside, exploring her newfound sensuality even though she suspects another brief week together can only lead to heartbreak. Her home is here; Rush's is hundreds of miles away.

But the heart knows no time or distance. If Reena can redefine her definition of home, she'll find love is the greatest wild rush of all.

Hearts Are Wild Series

No More Talking (novella)

Dare You To (novella)

Mad Love

Boys Of Summer

Bondi Beach Boys

Sand, Surf And Sunnie

Only You Series

All Of You

Holiday Romances

Christmas Wishes

New Year's Kisses

Valentine's Dates

Secret Santa

Frosty's Snowmen Series

A Touch Of Frost

A Kiss From Kringle

A Taste For Kandy

Secret Confessions

Sydney Housewives – Virginia

Standalone Titles

Make You Burn

PARANORMAL ROMANCE

Coyote Hunger Series

Coyote Home

Coyote Wild

Coyote Whispers

Coyote Law (novella)

Coyote Lies

For a full list of available books visit

http://www.rhiancahill.com/books/

For what's coming next, latest releases, sales and more, join

Rhian's Royal Readers

http://www.rhiancahill.com/contact/newsletter/